The Lion's Daughter

By the same author

Flaming Janet
Shadow of Palaces
Marjorie of Scotland
Here Lies Margot
Maddalena
Forget Not Ariadne
Julia
The Devil of Aske
The Malvie Inheritance
The Incumbent
Whitton's Folly
Norah Stroyan
The Green Salamander
Tsar's Woman
Homage to a Rose
Stranger's Forest
Daneclere
Daughter of Midnight
Fire Opal
Knock at a Star
A Place of Ravens
This Rough Beginning
The House of Cray
The Fairest One of All
Duchess Cain
Bride of Ae
The Copper-Haired Marshal
Still Blooms the Rose
The Governess
Children of Lucifer

Sable for the Count
My Lady Glamis
Venables
The Sisters
Digby
Fenfallow
The Sutburys
Jeannie Urquhart
The Woman in the Cloak
Artemia
Trevithick
The Loves of Ginevra
Vollands
A Dark Star Passing
The Brocken
The Sword and the Flame
Mercer
The Silver Runaways
Angell & Sons
Aunt Lucy
O Madcap Duchess
The Parson's Children
The Man from the North
Journey Beyond Innocence
The Charmed Descent
The Inadvisable Marriages
Curtmantle
Murder in Store
The Supplanter
Countess Isabel

The Lion's Daughter

PAMELA HILL

ROBERT HALE · LONDON

© Pamela Hill 1999
First published in Great Britain 1999

ISBN 0 7090 6468 3

Robert Hale Limited
Clerkenwell House
Clerkenwell Green
London EC1R 0HT

The right of Pamela Hill to be identified as
author of this work has been asserted by her
in accordance with the Copyright, Designs and
Patents Act 1988.

2 4 6 8 10 9 7 5 3 1

Typeset in North Wales by
Derek Doyle & Associates, Mold, Flintshire.
Printed in Great Britain by
St Edmundsbury Press, Bury St Edmunds, Suffolk.
Bound by WBC Book Manufacturers Limited, Bridgend

I

1

'Meggotta'.

I can hear my husband's deep voice saying it, with the long vowels of Norfolk which he never lost. As soon as she could speak, our daughter had made the name for herself out of Margaret, which is mine. When her father played with her he began to echo it, and soon we used it even in despatches to the king. Meggotta. It delighted me to watch my husband Hubert's face, worn with long trouble, screw up in lines of boyish pleasure again as the tiny creature laughed up at him. He adored her, the only child I bore him. I was thirty-four years old by the time we married, and Hubert, whom they made earl of Kent then, was twenty years older than I. It was a lasting wonder and joy to both of us when I conceived at once and gave birth safely.

Margaret is an old Scots royal name. My bastard half-sister, or rather one of them, has it also. So did an aunt, father's sister, who was married into Brittany in the days when Scots princesses began to be sought as brides abroad. By my time, it was different.

I and my next sister Isabel – there were two of those as well, but the other in the family was twice married before I was born – were sent into England as hostages when I was twenty-one years old. The reason was explained to me by my father, King William the Lion, when he rode abroad with me as he often did, and the great rampant device of Scotland above us flaunting its gules and or to tell everyone the king rode out, and would hear petitions. That day he did not stop to consider any, but rode straight with me at his side to the chapel at Dunfermline, which my mother the queen had once again made rich with embroideries since the troubles. Inside were tombs. Father left his mount with the grooms, took my hand and went with me to where the candles burned at the head and the foot of the dead, who were royal and the chapel's founders. One I already knew of was King Malcolm III, who had reigned in the Conqueror's time and that of his son. The other tomb was of his wife Margaret, who had been so beautiful that King Malcolm insisted on marrying her after her ship was cast on the coast of Fife in a storm. She had been of the old royal house of England, and was his second wife.

My father laid his hand on the tomb of King Malcolm, who has been described in a poem as the best king who ever ruled in Alban, which was soon after called Scotia. 'I would speak with you, Mag,' he said, using the name he always had for me and which nobody else, not even Hubert, used later on. I looked up at the Lion's face, by then the face of an old man; he had married late and ruled long, and had seen much war and bitterness. He was a tall long-legged Norman, for his mother Countess Ada had been a de Warenne from the south; and he was not handsome, like the lost and beautiful king his older brother, my dead young uncle Malcolm IV. I had seen Malcolm's likeness on a painted capital in company with his grandfather, King David, grey of beard as my father would be now if he wore one; but father was clean-shaven in the Norman fashion. When the Lion was younger his hair had been brown in colour, like mine; but his brother Malcolm the Maiden, as they called him because he had taken a vow of chastity, had had fair hair, and that silver-fair colour had come down to several of us from the Saxon inheritance, not only from Malcolm III's queen Margaret Atheling but later, by way of her son King David's queen, who had been a daughter of Earl Waltheof, son of Siward, and that goes back to certain fabled ancestry in Northumbria.

It was of that province that my father talked now. 'We have always craved it because of the good port of Berwick, which deals with much of our trade. I remember first seeing it when old King David rode down with me as a boy, and acknowledged all the bustle. Lacking that, the nearest is the shipping centre at Inverness, and further north to Moray.' His eyes grew distant, and I know he was remembering those flat far northern places and deep glens where he and my uncle David of Huntingdon, even in the days of vassaldom, had ridden to build strong forts at east and west. Father remembered me at last instead, and smiled down, his long face lightening beneath the plain round cap. He seldom needed to wear armour now, and the great cloak across his shoulders was that of a religious order. He used to jest about the fact that in places like Germany, they wrote of him already as William the Holy. He had had his unholy times nevertheless, as he admitted.

'You know, Mag, that you are the heir to Scotland if any harm should come to your brother. God forbid that that should happen. However, in Scotland we remember a woman's good rule, my mother's. Ada the Countess was regent for her son my brother Malcolm four years, quelling rebellions in Galloway and Moray and the border. She was widowed and had no aid. You have the wisdom to do as she did, but also the courage to go as hostage on behalf of your brother now. I am anxious that he should succeed in peace when I come to die.'

I made the sign of the cross, for though I loved the Lion I loved still more my little brother Alexander, now aged ten. I had loved him since he had first grasped my finger with his baby fist. He had red hair.

'My sending you into England is not a light matter,' continued the king. 'It grieves me that I may not soon see you more, or Isabel, whom I am sending with you for your comfort. If I do this, King John, who is descended from the devil like his sire, will come and go on the matter of the northern shires when I meet with him soon at Norham.'

I nodded. The thought of going to England was not strange to me, for many of our Scots lords had lands there, especially my uncle David, father's youngest brother who rode often up to his place of Lindores in Fife from his other one near

Northampton. He and his wife Maud were hospitable and kindly, and would see that Isabel and I were well treated. My uncle David had himself been a hostage in his youth. I did not need to say any of this to the king.

'Will it be soon?' was all I asked. I knew my mother would weep at parting, also that she would insist on preparing our gear as was fitting for princesses. She had a sense of what was proper despite having been no more than the daughter of a Norman viscount, married to my father on the instructions of Henry II. The wedding at Woodstock had been a grand one, but father was a reluctant bridegroom. Since the birth, at last, of Alexander after myself, Isabel and young Marjory, he had however begun to appreciate my mother's wisdom and piety, and had stopped taking mistresses.

'It will not now be till early August,' replied the king concerning Norham. 'It will take the devil's grandson a long time to get there, having seized the property of all his clergy following the late interdict.'

I knew that it would trouble my mother Queen Ermengarde that there would be no church services in the ordinary way now in England; where we lived, such matters had gone on as usual, for since the disagreement early in my father's reign, Scotland had been under the special protection of the pope. However babies could be christened in England and dead folk buried; they could hardly be denied the favour.

We rode back, and on the way I pondered the matter of father's name. He had of course been christened William after the old de Warennes, kin to my grandmother and earls of

Warren and Surrey in the south since the reign of Rufus; but the Lion is a name taken by several rulers including the late King Richard, from whom father bought back Scotland's freedom in 1189 when the Lion Heart wanted money for his wars in the Holy Land. That blotted out the shame of Falaise, where father, taken prisoner earlier in Northumbria, had been compelled to sign a treaty of homage to Henry II if he ever wanted to regain his freedom. My uncle David had been captured also, and neither of them had wives then, or heirs.

Henry II was called the lion's whelp, from an old prophecy which also called his grandfather, Henry I Beauclerc, the Lion of Justice. All these lions contrived a certain firm rule and good laws, but my young uncle Malcolm the Maiden died at twenty-four of a phthisis caught following Henry II's Welsh campaigns. He admired Henry almost as a god, and did his bidding even to the extent of handing back Huntingdon and Northampton – which had come to old King David by marriage – without making conditions. Malcolm IV's brothers, and his subjects, were not pleased. At one time, before the civil war in England between the Lion of Justice's daughter Maud and her cousin Stephen, who had seized the crown, King Stephen, who was a kind-hearted man with a muddled head, gave Huntingdon away while it still belonged to us, and in compensation offered the king of Scots Northumbria and Cumbria, including Carlisle. It was there that my grandmother Ada de Warenne and King David's son, Earl Henry, were married. Earl Henry himself, who would have made a good king of Scots, died of fever in the year before his father

King David, leaving my uncle Malcolm to inherit while no more than a boy. All that is well known; and the troubles that followed caused my father to raise the Lion standard at last as a means of rallying the different races that made up his kingdom when his brother Malcolm died. Gaels, Norsemen and Flemings in the north-east, sons of the old Picts who were no longer named, the men of Strathclyde and Galloway, the Anglo-Normans of Lothian, and the border clans and the rest could rally to the Lion wherever it flew, and may do so one day even if there is no king in Scotland. It was not, therefore, a personal name of father's or any way of vaunting himself. It was a precaution for the future.

2

Isabel and I did not ride to Norham on the brown deep-running Tweed, as we were to be bargained for. Instead, we sat with my mother and the other Isabel, who had come north to us in Edinburgh on a visit, drinking Gascony wine. Isabel's husband Robert de Ros made a good sum of money yearly despite the king of England's tax, which he evaded when he could, by sending wool out from the Humber and getting this wine back. He had sent us a tun with Isabel, and very good it was. She knew, of course, what was taking place at Norham, and was a person who always said what she thought. She was the daughter of an Eskdale woman with whom my father had been greatly taken up in youth, and was older than most of us. Her first husband had been Robert de Brus, who had lands in Skelton, but they had had no children. I was glad her present husband was not with her, despite his gift of wine; he was a man who made a great deal of noise and was always ready to take the opposite view. I am like my mother the queen in that I believe in peace and quiet, and she sat now saying little, her shrewd Beaumont features serene, sipping cautiously. She herself had lion's blood, though on the wrong side of the blanket, being descended from one of King Henry Beauclerc's seventeen illegitimate daughters, all of whom he had seen married well.

'I have no doubt the other Margaret and de Vesci will be at Norham,' Isabel de Ros said. 'They can never miss an occasion, and the prince of Wales they say is to be present, having made peace with his father-in-law for the time.'

This Llewelyn ap Iowerth's father-in-law was none other than the English king, though again on the wrong side of the blanket; the Welsh prince had been married to John's bastard daughter Joan for the sake of goodwill, but she had spoiled it by being unfaithful and her lover, one of the de Braose family, had been hanged by the vengeful husband. It was an advance that Llewelyn had agreed to come to Norham in company with King John.

My own sister Isabel chimed in, 'I hope the little king of England – like many small men he is lecherous, as you know – will not cast an eye on our other Margaret in his accustomed fashion. Eustace would be troublesome.' Eustace de Vesci was a fiercely possessive husband, my half-sister Margaret being a most desirable woman. Shortly my mother's third daughter by the king, my sister Marjory, would become one also; she was as beautiful as anyone I have ever seen, and sat now with the summer sun on her hair, doing nothing, and silent, because she already knew there was nothing she need do but let others look at her. Watching her as I liked to, I knew I was seeing the lost silver-fair beauty of Earl Henry and Earl Waltheof; of Malcolm the Maiden, of Margaret Atheling herself; perhaps of that other Margaret my father's sister, who had married into Brittany and there given birth to a daughter named Constance. Henry II had married the little Constance to his son Geoffrey, and they in turn had a son named Arthur and a daughter named Eleanor, both with the silver-gilt hair and sea-blue eyes no one who had seen them could forget. It was unknown what had become of Arthur since King John had laid hold of him seven or eight years ago and put him in prison; he had a better claim than John to the crown of England, which almost certainly meant that he was murdered. His sister Eleanor was kept in England in confinement; they had called her the Pearl of Brittany and it was unlikely she would ever be set free.

I shivered, not liking to think of father's riding to Norham to face any such king; but there would be no treachery while Alexander was safe with us in Edinburgh. My father greatly desired that Alexander should succeed him peacefully, and to that end would come and go, in his own phrase, with the English usurper. John had, apart from Arthur, done his best to ensure that his elder brother King Richard would never come out of his Austrian prison, but it had happened, and John had been forgiven, and soon an arrow had finished off Richard in any case at Chaluz. There was no doubt now who ruled England, well enough now it was his; and it was wise of my father to treat with him for the sake of the heir.

*

Matters seemed to have sped at Norham amicably enough, as we heard later, and all parties thereafter rode their separate ways; but I heard later still that King John had indeed slid between the bed-curtains to Margaret de Vesci in her husband's absence, and she had known no difference in the dark. Eustace was thereafter the English king's deadly enemy, as might have been foreseen. Meantime, we two young women said farewell to our mother and the assembled family, though Isabel de Ros rode back with us to her own. We had the escort, as far as Durham, of my father's bastard son Robert of London, whom father had defiantly brought north on his saddle-bow shortly after his wedding to my mother, having already left her to make her entry into Edinburgh alone. There was none of that unhappiness remaining now, and mother had from the beginning been kindness itself to all of the Lion's family already got. She had grieved sincerely when young Ada, who had been married to the earl of Dunbar, had died; I myself was by then present, aged fourteen. Before Alexander's birth my mother no doubt found it hard to accept that of a second son called Henry, born to a woman of Ibrox when father rode that way in our childhood. We saw less of Henry than of Robert, who had grown up as our elder brother, and nothing at all of little Africa, whose mother kept her to herself.

I was sad at leaving, and especially so at parting with Alexander, who had received the homage of the assembled

Scots lords at Musselburgh with great dignity when he was three. He was the same now, unperturbed and sensible. However as small boys will, he doubled up his fists and swore to come and fight the English if they mistreated me. I had perhaps been more of a mother to him than a sister, with my own mother so greatly engaged in pious works and in being a stepmother. For whatever reason, Alexander was fond of me. 'Have no fear,' I said to him. 'Isabel and I are going to learn courtly dances, and how to behave in great company.'

'There is great enough company here. It is a pity you have to go.'

In fact young Isabel was looking forward to it, and so in a way was I. The queen of England was exactly my own age, and said to be beautiful; King John had fallen in love with her in the Angoumois when she was eleven. Marjory in fact was envious of us both, and hoped to join us as a third hostage at Woodstock when she was older.

We were to be met meantime at Durham by an escort of my uncle David's, who would have come himself except that he was engaged in marrying his eldest daughter, yet another Margaret, to the lord of Galloway, who had ridden south after the assembly at Norham. The feasting would be notable, and the marriage itself was a relief, as the men of Galloway had been the first to desert my father at the time of Falaise, and had mounted a rebellion in their accustomed fashion, wearing their eelskin belts. They are neither flesh nor fowl there, being a sliver of land jutting out on its own and almost considering itself a separate kingdom. The lord Alan by now was however my uncle's son-in-law, and would be our ally. He was somewhat older than the bride, who was nineteen and his second wife. However perhaps she would cause him in some way to settle down.

We came to Durham, and visited the great cathedral there, but to my disappointment were not allowed, as women, to go near the tomb of St Cuthbert. That was odd, as the saint had had many friends in his lifetime who were women, and one of them had woven his shroud. The fine shroud had adhered to his face when they opened the coffin long after in the time of my great-uncle Alexander, who later on reigned in Scotland before his brother David and alongside his brother Edgar. Alexander – they called him the Fierce for no reason except one chase of rebels across a river in spate in the north – had made a gift of Turkish armour brought home from the Holy Land, and a horse with silver trappings, which he had led up to the altar at Durham. The horse was long gone, but we saw the armour gleaming, and the trappings laid by it. It took one back in time. Afterwards Isabel spoke to me in a hushed voice when we were again outside in the daylight.

'They say the saint himself was incorrupt, having been dead more than five hundred years,' she said. 'The abbot of Séez sat him up and pulled at his ears and feet. Robert told me.'

'Robert was not there,' I said drily. I recalled instead the pleasing tale of how St Cuthbert had been used to undergo secret penances by standing all night in the cold sea off Lindisfarne, and in the morning a pair of sea otters – he greatly loved animals – would come and dry his feet with their fur. When he found that this had been discovered the saint was greatly vexed; he liked to be solitary, and ended his days as a hermit on Inner Farne, having been unwillingly made a bishop. I like the animal stories of his founder St Columba also; Columba knew when a sick bird would land on Iona and warned his monks to tend it when it came. Churchmen are no longer that gentle and agreeable way inclined, being too greatly concerned with their own advancement and with obeying Rome. I have nothing to say about the pope except that he is a long way off and as liable, therefore, to make mistakes as any other man. I often wonder if my ancestress Margaret Atheling, once she was King Malcolm's queen and he would do anything she said, might not have been better to let well alone with the Columban church in Scotland. She was not greatly liked there for her Roman reforms. The old Culdee monks – they were given the name later by way of Germany – are still to be found, I believe, in remote places in Moray and in the deep forests; some were flushed out by my great-grandfather King David when he was building one of his abbeys near Selkirk. However there is nothing I myself may do about such things, and I have known many good and holy men in the church in England; the best of them was Archbishop Stephen Langton, whom King John once threatened to hang for obeying the pope.

We rode down through England itself, having seen Robert of London back to the north and being met, instead, by my uncle

David's two bastard sons, Henry of Brechin and Henry of Stirling, both for the time in the south. The name was of course from their mutual grandfather, Earl Henry; but he in turn had been named for King Henry Beauclerc, who had sheltered King David in his young days and given him a rich bride. The two Henries guided us at last to Yardley Chase, past other great forests which at that time of year were turning their colours. I noted the poor folk avoiding them, for they dared not be suspected of stealing so much as a hare for the pot in England or they would lose their sight, their right hand or their testicles. Those were the cruel forest laws of the Norman kings, which in Scotland could not have been carried out. Otherwise, King John was said to be just to the poor, and to ride up and down the land far more than his father or his brother had done, dispensing the laws. He had by then lost Normandy, which gave him more leisure for his kingdom.

3

My uncle David welcomed us, and there were enough cold meats left from the wedding-feast to satisfy our hunger. His house could be called a palace, and was of great magnificence, like everything about him; when he had ridden down the spine of the Pennines to war with Henry II long ago while my father harried the north-east before Falaise, it had been with painted shields and bright banners. Everything in my uncle's house was rich and beautiful, including his young wife, Maud of Chester. She was a daughter of old Earl Ranulf, and it had been a shrewd move on the part of my uncle David to secure her as soon as Henry II was dead and he could choose a wife for himself. Earl Ranulf had in his time fallen out with King David over which of them possessed Carlisle. My father's brother Earl David of Huntingdon – he had regained the title owing to the tactful death without heirs of the earlier claimant – was a princely figure now even in old age. He was full of stories, some of them from the East. He had had many adventures there, and could talk about Coeur de Lion and Saladin and the way the emperor Isaac Comnenus was put in silver chains by King Richard on Cyprus, as he had begged not to have to endure iron ones. That had been the somewhat cruel humour of the Lion Heart, who had neglected his new queen Berengaria to make love instead to a little child, the emperor's daughter. King John had also stayed late in bed each day with his bride of eleven; and they said old Henry II had seduced young Alais of France, intended for his son. All that is long-dead gossip now, but it describes the way of that family.

Earl David had lost two infant sons, I think because he insisted on taking Maud up to Lindores on each occasion to give them birth in Scotland. The third boy baby, not a taking creature, had been safely born in Yardley and, with equal regard for safety, named John. Otherwise there were Isabella and Ada, younger than we were; Margaret of course had already gone north-west to Galloway. The little girls ran about freely, their skirts whisking.

I admired the painted shields in Earl David's hall. 'There was a time when there were no devices, and nobody knew who was friend or enemy in war,' he replied, fingering a wrought silver cup with figures in enamel, showing the story of Tristram and Iseult. 'My father Earl Henry escaped by riding off among the English cavalry at Northallerton, with his visor down; had he been known he would have been killed. There are two sides to the matter, in such ways.' He stared into the cup.

His countess appeared and laid a hand on the old earl's elegant sleeve. 'My lord, the princesses will be tired; they have come a long way.'

Had she known, we had further by far to go.

We did not sleep at once, but fell to counting on our fingers, like two children, the number of Margarets and Isabels and Henries and Adas in all of our family. Even one of the poor little dead babies at Lindores had been christened Henry in time.

'It will be simpler when we meet the de Warenne kin,' my sister said. 'They are always called William.'

I knew my father had informed the sixth earl Warren, his second cousin, that we were to come to court, in the hope that that personage, who always sought favour, would obtain some for us there. It was in this way, later on, that I first heard the name of the man who was to become my husband. Hubert de Burgh had been considered privileged to be allowed to marry a widowed cousin of the earl's, who had been born a de Warenne but had married a Bardolf. There had been one son, William as expected, and now the lady Beatrice and the knight Hubert de Burgh had another son named John. All that was in Norfolk, where the earl had great estates. So had the Bigods, one of whom was to become my brother-in-law many years after.

Meantime, having rested at Yardley, we were taken further south to court, at Woodstock for the time.

*

The court was full of young people, for the king liked all his nobles to send their sons and daughters into his charge. This was partly to ensure their parents' obedience, but in the nature of things the court itself was a light-hearted place despite the rumour that the queen had once taken a lover of low birth and that the king had found out, and hanged the man over the frame of her bed like Llewelyn ap Iowerth. Queen Isabella by now was, as I have said, my own age, and busy bearing the king's children; the heir, Prince Henry, was a thin fair child of two. However one noblewoman, Matilda de Braose, had refused to send her sons to the king, saying openly that he was not to be trusted after having murdered his own nephew Arthur of Brittany. No one but the lady de Braose would have spoken out to such an extent, and she paid for it dearly with a most terrible death by starvation. Seeing the king, it was difficult to picture him as responsible for as much as rumour credited, such as having sent a poisoned egg to a young woman who refused to lie with him, so that her bowels turned to water till she died. No doubt the fact that the king was excessively fond of eggs gave rise to the story. However Matilda de Braose was certainly starved to death at Windsor later on, along with her son, whose dead flesh she is said to have gnawed at last in desperate hunger: but my mind grasps at evil if I do not prevent it. The king, as expected, was a small ugly dark man with broad shoulders, and nostrils that flared like a bull's. They did not dilate notably at the sight of either Isabel or myself, and so we thankfully avoided the fate of my half-sister Vesci in Northumbria. King John liked to wear a great many jewels, perhaps to make himself noticeable. The queen, on the other hand, dressed plainly: even her coronation gown was remembered as having been merely of scarlet and grey cloth, such as anyone might have worn. Isabella of Angoulême's chief beauty was her glorious golden hair, which is perhaps what had attracted the king in the first place, or else it was her youth. By now, she disliked him and no doubt bore his children unwillingly. Yet John had charm; his dead father, Henry II, had preferred him above all his sons, and had died of a broken heart at Chinon on hearing of his betrayal.

John had also, as I have said, betrayed his brother Richard, who forgave him for having delayed his ransom and tried to usurp his throne, then named him on his deathbed as to inherit after all, instead of Arthur; unless that is a tale, like so much else. All I know is that I myself did not dislike the king as much as I had expected to do. We saw, in fact, little of him, as he was forever journeying up and down England, which alarmed his barons, used as they had hitherto been, in the late reign, to do much as they chose, with nobody to witness their misdeeds who would be listened to. King John saw and heard things for himself, and championed the poor.

4

The interdict in England, present on our arrival, affected the ordinary people very little, as they held services in the open air and this, perhaps, gave some the notion that it could be done anyway. We ourselves were able to attend masses in convent churches, as these had a dispensation to be allowed to continue behind closed doors. However the whole arrangement had the drawback that it did not deter or disturb the king, who went on as he had formerly done, in official sin and detriment. Like his forebear Rufus, he had declined the sacrament at his first coronation, and there were whispers that he worshipped Rufus's forest gods. Certainly John was devoted to the hunt, and rode out often and furiously. I dislike hunting, though I greatly enjoy riding at speed; but the excitement of the chase ends there for me, and I hate seeing the brave stag brought down in its blood, pulled at by dogs, killed and gutted and borne back on poles at last with its feet tied after valiant running. I love all animals, and like best to walk through a forest alone, seeing the rabbits scuttle in the grass and the red squirrels chatter up trees, and the primroses in season making a creamy carpet.

However to return to the king, he was excommunicated in person no more than weeks after our arrival, and excommunication is a far more serious matter than an interdict. It affects the king's own dignity, his very authority. No one is going to obey or respect a man who is cut off from receiving God; and it was about that time that certain barons contrived a plot to murder King John, which brought him hurrying back from Ireland and Wales, where he had made war again, and then peace, with Llewelyn.

There was trouble and wary dealing all of that year and the next, and we ourselves were little heeded and did not expect to be. However in the year following, we had the great joy of seeing Alexander, now aged fourteen, ride down to be knighted by the king at Clerkenwell. My brother had grown almost to be a man, not as tall as our father, but conspicuous with his red hair and his compact strength. Naturally he brought a strong following, who remained with him at the ceremony. I and Isabel, and Marjory who had taken the chance to be escorted down to join us, did not attend, being women, and it took place in the church of the celibate Knights of St John, present in numbers with their dark cloaks and great crosses argent. The king himself I believe wore white leather gauntlets with a sapphire on one and a ruby on the other. He was friendly to Alexander, which boded well. However it would not be long till he referred to our brother in despatches as the little red fox. The reason was Scotland's old allegiance to France.

This tale is not an easy one. My father, at the beginning of his reign – and he had in plain fact ruled before that while his sick brother Malcolm lay on his deathbed – had had reason to quarrel with Henry II, who had been protected by old King David earlier but showed no signs of gratitude, and behaved as though the Scots ought to consider themselves his vassals. He brought forward the old argument that King Malcolm III had sworn in his day to be the vassal of the Conqueror, Henry's great-grandfather. This is not the case, as my father the Lion himself made clear to me often. The Conqueror indeed marched north in 1072, but the sight of the mountains beyond Abernethy defeated him, even as the Romans had been defeated earlier and further south. King Malcolm Ceann Mór – this means Great Chief, never Big Head as folk down here seem to think – swore to aid King William in war, in other words to be his 'man' if he should be in difficulties. This is a very different thing from putting Scotland under vassalage, and at that early time the different tribes who made up the future kingdom would not have understood the word, let alone agreed with it. Nevertheless the notion persisted among the Norman and Angevin kings who succeeded in England, but Henry II, unsuccessful also in Wales, had to abandon his notion of being overlord of the whole island called Britain, even though he insisted that he was the descendant of its original discoverer, Brute.

About or before 1170, my father made a visit to France. He

greatly hoped for an alliance with the French king, Louis VII, and he was not disappointed.

It so happened that Louis had unwittingly lost the lands which he had gained through his marriage to the heiress of Aquitaine, whom he had divorced as she bore him no sons. Henry of Anjou, not yet king of England, at once snapped up the discarded Eleanor, who promptly bore him five sons including King John. It was not only that episode that left Louis VII with a grievance – he had never, in the first place, wanted to part with Eleanor at all – but by the new marriage, especially when Henry II inherited the English throne on the death of King Stephen, France was surrounded by the lands of the powerful Angevin and, herself, forced to shrink to a small area round Paris. Even Normandy belonged to Henry, with its ports and rivers, owing to the short-sighted gift, to certain disturbing Norse pirates, of an earlier king of the Franks.

It suited my father and Louis, therefore, to make an alliance against the king of England. Scots and French have since then continued to agree – in Lothian then, even the language was the same – and father's later capture in Northumbria, and imprisonment in Falaise, was the result of an arrangement with Louis VII to make war on Henry II in three directions, all of which failed.

Scotland by now was free again, however, and there was no question of any vassalage from Alexander, now or in the future. Lands held in England by Scots nobles, even the king, were a different matter, and homage was never refused by us for those. However Henry II at the bitter time just after Falaise had tried to include the very church in Scotland, saying it must be subject to the see of York. My father was compelled then, before being allowed to return to his kingdom, to perform a second act of homage to a particularly unpleasant archbishop named Roger of Pont l'Evêque, who made the most of the occasion. However the pope sent legates to Edinburgh after father's return – King Henry did his utmost to prevent their passage through England – and it was decided that the church in Scotland was free and independent of any see but that of Peter. My father later received the Golden Rose, a sign of papal favour; I remember seeing its delicate wrought gold branches and petals, set with gleaming sapphires, the royal gem.

Now, England under King John was in deep trouble with the new pope, who was a masterful man of thirty-seven at the time of his election, at which time he had taken the name of Innocent III. Pope Innocent personally elected an archbishop of Canterbury, to the fury of the king, who had other candidates. No doubt John had his own point of view in such matters; in the days of old the Saxon kings chose their own primate without reference to Rome. Since then, however, the Normans had consistently quarrelled with their archbishops and on several occasions had sent them packing abroad; this had happened more than once with the saintly Anselm and, famously, with Thomas Becket.

Stephen Langton, the pope's choice after a feud concerning two others, was the best possible answer in all ways. He was devout, a scholar and theologian, had written magnificent prayers, could argue knowledgeably in council, and was physically most worthy of the office, being tall and broad of shoulder, with a noble and dignified bearing and a pleasant face. Later I was to talk with him often. The king had at first refused to receive him, then had forced him abroad, and now, with humiliations piling up from all directions, at last knelt to Stephen Langton publicly, received absolution from him and, in the next month, had the interdict in England lifted by the pope's legate, the bishop of Tusculum. Bells rang joyfully, but six years without official services had maybe put in the minds of certain folk that they had contrived without them and gone on living. Others murmured at the sight of a king of England kneeling to a foreigner. The wrong was put right, but it was mortifying for the little king, and the whole matter had done harm from the beginning and had lessened John's authority by the end.

In general, it could be understood why certain of the English barons had already made overtures to the son of King Philip Augustus of France, himself the successor, got at last by a third marriage, of old Louis VII, long dead. Before the settlement the pope had invited Philip Augustus himself to invade England. By now, with matters settled at Rome, that monarch was canny, earned his sobriquet given him for wisdom, and stayed at home. His son Louis was a different matter, and one way and another Alexander my brother was drawn in; for sad reasons.

News came of the Lion's death at Stirling, in 1214. I had

hoped to embrace my father again, and now it would not happen. I think it was then that England began to be my home.

My father had reigned almost fifty years, and no doubt all of us expected him to live forever. However he must have been old and tired, and had black memories. He was buried, in the great cloak of the order to which he had lately vowed himself, in the abbey he had founded at Arbroath in honour of St Thomas Becket. As that saint had directly caused father's earlier capture at Alnwick after the penance of Henry II for involvement in his murder, this seemed an odd choice at the time; perhaps father respected Becket's known dislike of the insufferable Roger of York. For whatever reason, there the old Lion rests his bones, within sound of the sea, and may they rest in peace. Alexander II was king.

I wrote consolation to my mother, who elected to stay in Scotland. She had made many friends there by her kindness and good works, and had endowments in which she took a practical interest. Also, no doubt she felt it her duty to pray for my father's soul, and the political uncertainties in England might still, at any time, prevent such prayers from officially reaching God.

The discontented barons no doubt used the pope's former eagerness that France should invade England, appealing not to King Philip who, the pope's obedient son as stated, disapproved of the venture after the reconciliation and lifting the interdict, but to his young heir Louis. Prince Louis had an additional goad in his wife, a ruthless and strong-minded young woman chosen for him by her maternal grandmother, no other than Henry II's widow, Eleanor of Aquitaine. The old lady, shortly before her death at about eighty years of age, had journeyed on a mule to Spain for the purpose of inspecting the various princesses available to France, and instead of the one expected, whose name she said the French would be unable to pronounce, she had selected another sister, Blanche. Blanche was perhaps her grandmother's image, except for extreme piety. Eleanor herself had never been permitted by either of her husbands to rule, even in her own duchy; but she had that ability as well as others. She must have seen in this girl herself as she might have been, and young Prince Louis, the bridegroom, as wax for the moulding, more than could have been said for the late Henry II.

Blanche proved fertile; there was already not one heir of the marriage but two; and Prince Louis, no doubt taken with the notion of invading England and wresting the kingdom from his friend Arthur of Brittany's killer, had the double excuse of having been invited to come by the English baronage, or some of it, and the supposed right of inheritance of his wife Blanche as a granddaughter of Henry II. She herself was warlike enough to supply her husband continuously with arms from across the Channel. Soon, much of the south-east was in Louis' hands, and one lord who joined him, thinking all else lost, was my kinsman of Warren and Surrey.

Whether the English would have been better or worse off had the French invasion been successful and Blanche of Castile been crowned queen of England and France, nobody can say. What befell shortly at Runnymede might have been different, or might not have happened at all. Meantime one man who helped to prevent the success of the French, holding Dover Castle despite a long and bitter siege by sea and land, was my own beloved husband-to-be, Hubert de Burgh; one of the greatest men ever to achieve power in England.

I have said very little about Hubert up till now; he was never the kind of man whose presence requires trumpets. He was quiet and dependable, and strong Dover held out valiantly in his charge all through the months when young Louis was in England, had most of the south-east, and was in touch with my brother Alexander in the north parts. The west remained in John's hands. Meantime it behoves me to say a little more about our bustling relative, the sixth earl of Warren and Surrey.

He had sought favour, respectability, and sheriffdoms from his youth, being afflicted with shame because his father had been an illegitimate half-brother of Henry II: he himself had changed his name back to his mother's. Cognatus Regis – the earl became known by this sobriquet because he kept close to the side of the king and, in time, the king's son when crowned – was married first to a bride from the Albini family of Arundel, but fancied a mistress in the Marches, prudently far from court. She bore him a son and a daughter, and the daughter became one of King John's concubines. No doubt her sire was gratified; it was one step higher on the ladder. The son who was born was known as Richard Fitzroy, and he had his royal father's ambition in no small degree, also a strong moneymaking streak; he grew to be one of the richest men in the kingdom, by what means I know not; it may be that he indulged in some enterprise like de Ros with his wool and wine on the Humber, or de Vesci – who had fled abroad – by a port built earlier at Alnmouth which prospered in a mild way till the king annexed it. However it happened, Richard Fitzroy was the hero of a famous episode, namely the killing at sea of the notorious Monk of Flanders.

The Monk, far from being engaged in his spiritual exercises, was the chief cause of the delay in raising the siege of Dover, where Hubert had held out now with his garrison for the best part of a year. The Monk for long challenged the shipping of England with a variable fleet of his own, and a fixed determination that Louis of France should become king of the English, no doubt with himself as archbishop. I know little of winds and tides; but Richard Fitzroy in some manner caused the favourable wind to lie with his veering ships, boarded the Monk's ship at last by grappling, found the Monk down in his cabin on his knees for once, and beheaded him. The head was set on a pole and paraded through the southern counties, then sent, a choice and malodorous gift, to the king. The menace in the Channel was removed; Louis went home to his pious Castilian wife and soon became king of France; and Hubert de Burgh at last rode out of Dover.

I can remember a strange thing, no doubt occurring out of its place in time in my mind. Upon news of the interdict, all of the bishops had earlier left England, their defiant mitres like so many sails drawing out from harbour in the prevailing offshore wind. As I have said, life went on without them; in its way it resembled the simpler days of the Columbans, with monks only as priests, no princes; though Columba himself had been of royal blood, the great-grandson of Niall of the Nine Hostages, and when a battle was fought for his rights in Ireland and caused much bloodshed, he reproached himself and left the beloved land, coming instead to a small island from which he could no longer see it. The men of Erin love forever and hate forever. One way and another we contrived in England without the bishops, but there was one who remained.

I saw him ride one day through Winchester, which by bad chance had perhaps by then become his see. He rode proudly, as though he owned England. I had a sensation of evil passing, but thought it might be the general absence of blessings and of the safe, known things of the church of God we were denied in England then. Why Peter des Roches was a churchman except for ambition I know not, and granted he was neither the first nor the last to be tonsured for the sake of rising in the world. He was a Poitevin, and at that time that was all I had heard. I was one day to learn much more, to my grief; but not yet.

The sixth earl had meanwhile made his lifetime's mistake and had declared openly for Prince Louis. King John never forgave him while he lived. However John Lackland would not live long, though events were to follow his progress relentlessly to the end.

Altogether there had been no time for anyone to consider the question of our marriages, Isabel's and mine and Marjory's, for my youngest and most beautiful sister had ridden down at the friendlier time when Alexander was knighted, and stayed on with us. Her marvellous beauty continued to turn heads, but the French alliance discouraged proposals from anyone of prudence in England or elsewhere after it became evident that Prince Louis would have to go home.

5

I once had speech with King John alone, at a time when I had thought him elsewhere. I was in the habit of going now and again to mass at Godstow when the court was at Woodstock, for I had been able to hear it there all through the time of the interdict, behind closed doors. Now, all could come; it must have been after the joy-bells had been rung, but likewise after the disastrous battle at Bouvines, in which the king had lost to Philip Augustus virtually all he had retained in France. I remember it was late autumn, and the chapel was cold. I saw a small broad-shouldered figure standing alone before a certain tomb. I had come up to him before I knew it was the king; he wore a hood. The face he turned to me was one of deep bitterness, more than I have ever seen in any man, even my husband after his fall from office. John's hair and beard had turned white early, as happens with some; but his face remained smooth, as though trouble could not touch it in any lasting fashion.

'Have you come to triumph over me, Margaret of

Scotland?' he asked and returned to contemplation of the tomb. It was that of Fair Rosamund Clifford, who had been a nun here for years after she ended her liaison with Henry II, having borne him two sons. One entered the church and was with his father at Chinon when Henry died. The other was William, earl of Salisbury, a man loyal to the king, and who had lately won a small victory, as such things are measured, at Damme, a Flemish port, taking much booty from the ships.

I replied truly that I had come to pray, but if I disturbed him I would go. At the same time I noted that the gold cloth and fresh flowers, with which the good sisters keep the tomb supplied despite an earlier bishop's remonstrance that they should cease to honour a whore, were removed today, perhaps by the king's order; they had obediently taken the dead woman's coffin out once already to the common graveyard, but afterwards had reverently brought it back when the bishop had gone. There was a mocking epitaph carved in the stone which I had not before seen, for the gold cloth usually covered it. *Once rose of the world, now a stinking heap of bones.* It was in convoluted Latin. King John excelled in languages, being said to speak nine.

'I had it carved there. That woman should have been queen of England,' said John Lackland. 'I and my brothers, great Eleanor's sons, were no more than bastards. Our father said as much before he died. He married Rosamund Clifford in his youth, in the Brecon country, when he was still uncertain of the throne. They had the two sons of their marriage.

Afterwards, as duke of Normandy and Anjou, he married my mother for her lands; he never loved her, or anyone in truth except the flesh that lies in there, if any remains.'

'He loved you,' I said. 'You were his favourite.'

'So I thought, but when I learned that saying of his that we were all of us bastards, and *her* sons the true heirs, I signed the treaty with my brothers that betrayed my father. That killed him, at Chinon. "Shame on a conquered king," he muttered, dying: so they told me. Maybe I will be able to say the same.'

'Maybe not,' I said, remembering how only that year, the determined little monarch, said by many to be a better soldier than his father and even his brother, had won back tricky Nantes and his dead father's capital of Angers, with its famed red-and-white towers and broad moat and high battlements; but after that the townsfolk would not fight with the king of England against the king of France, saying the last was their overlord. The real reason, as all knew, was the memory they had of a glorious young knight, Arthur of Brittany, aged sixteen, his fair hair shining where he stood on the battlements to receive their homage, twelve years back. They loved his courage and beauty, also the fact that by birth, being the son of John's elder brother Geoffrey, he was the rightful heir to Normandy, Anjou and England. I thought of Arthur now, and of how he had died. I was silent.

The murderer spoke once more before he turned away. 'Since I returned to God and his church, nothing has gone well for me,' he said, and left me staring uselessly at a dead woman's tomb.

There is a coldness in evil, and they say the deepest part of hell is deadly cold. They say also of John Lackland, now he is dead, that hell itself is defiled by his presence; but I never thought him worse that some. He had done murder, it is true, to his nephew, betrayed his brother Richard and their father; of all the magnificent sons of Eleanor and Henry II he seemed the worst and the last; but Richard was more cruel than he in Aquitaine, and as depraved in Cyprus. The Church, which damned Rufus, also damned the memory of John; and maybe for the same reason, that neither of them were Christian. Rufus had made no bones about it; John towards the end of his life turned to St Wulfstan, who may have saved him or else not. John's first marriage had been to a strange young woman who was herself pagan and of the descent of the great Robert of Gloucester, King Beauclerc's son, who should have been king himself but for his bastardy. Hadwisa of Gloucester was married young to the youngest prince, but the pope forbade the couple to live together because of consanguinity, regarding old Henry I. John was by then known for a fool, for at seventeen his doting father had tried to make him king in Ireland, but he and his friends pulled at the submissive chieftains' beards and made mock of them, causing ill feeling where there had been goodwill. John was brought home, and the pope, behindhand with news as usual, sent a crown of peacock feathers much too late. Later still, John begged on his knees to be allowed to accept the offer of the crown of

Jerusalem, but by then even Henry II knew it was not to be considered, and forbade it.

Jerusalem may have lain near John's heart by then. He was a strange creature. He had always been overshadowed by his brothers; born late, by which time his parents no longer agreed; his father's love of him did not fully come till after the death of the eldest remaining brother, Henry. who had been crowned in Henry II's own lifetime after the manner of France; and John may have heard of the glory of the wars in the Holy Land, the selection of a king once Jerusalem was won with much bloodshed, and the way his own forebear, Robert Curthose, had declined the crown even though his taper had lit itself three times in the Church of the Holy Sepulchre among the waiting candidates; it was taken for a sign, but Curthose said he preferred to wait for the crown of England, which was by right his. He failed in that, as all know, and ended in prison while his brother Beauclerc took the crown. It is not wise to ignore portents.

John may well have wanted to win renown – he was a courageous fighter – after his Irish folly, to lose the repute of a wastrel, and govern, with a strong hand, the holy eastern kingdom, as England at that time showed no prospect of becoming his. God knows what he thought, or wanted; but he was not allowed to go, which made one more failure. Too many can make a man bitter and useless, and a woman as well. Perhaps then John Lackland turned to women, and to ill.

The divorce from Hadwisa of Gloucester meant that he kept her dower lands, a cunning device of the old king's, who seldom let anything go if he could help it. Nevertheless John parted with some portion of the rents to allow Hadwisa to marry Geoffrey de Mandeville, the then earl of Essex, fining him heavily instead. Essex had a reputation somewhat like the earlier Bellêmes, wicked and mysterious. Much may have been said about him that was untrue; but after he died I remember seeing his long coffin suspended from a tree, for he was not allowed Christian burial.

I glimpsed it as we rode by, from one place to another; and saw the court ladies cross themselves, and whisper to each other. This may have been during the interdict, or when its effects still remained; but there it was, and why hang a cered corpse in its coffin from a tree without reason?

However other things might have been or not, Essex was brutal to his wife. When he died Hadwisa was likewise dying, her head forever in a tremor from the late earl's constant blows, her wits confused, her body a cadaver's. I heard all this from Hubert, who out of pity, and perhaps ambition, his Warenne wife having lately died, married Hadwisa himself. She had been near the late king – John was newly dead by then – and they say never loved anyone else. Hubert had his way to make, with nothing still but his own strong arm, his reputation gained at Dover, and his small son John, who must be provided for.

'I did not touch Hadwisa,' he told me. 'She only lived a few weeks longer. She had known hell with de Mandeville and shabby treatment earlier. I saw that she was cared for, as nobody else would concern themselves. She spent her time keening for the late king. I remember the thin sound, coming forever through the wall.'

Long since, at the time of the divorce, John had become enamoured of the little girl of eleven he had seen in Angoulême. Isabelle the count's daughter was betrothed elsewhere, but her parents were John's vassals and dared not refuse her to him. He married her, took her to bed behind closed curtains in Bordeaux and would stay there at pleasure with her each day till noon. By the time I met her, he had long since sated himself, had had Isabelle crowned at Westminster and caused her to bear him an heir six years after, then others.

At the time of that marriage Arthur of Brittany had been still alive, captured and in charge of Hubert de Burgh. Hubert, ordered by the king to put out the boy's eyes and castrate him, would not; I heard later what happened then. Soon Arthur was taken away, and never again seen alive. Philip Augustus of France, knowing he must be dead, demanded his homage. One man, de Braose, who alone knew the manner of the death, was ruined by the king with all his family, and alone escaped abroad to die. My husband contrived to live.

It was the death of the great Marshal, guardian of the realm, in 1219, that gave Hubert his rise to power. He had already been elected justiciar in the last year of King John, at the time of the signing of the great charter. In those uncertain times he was the only man left in England, failing the Marshal, to be trusted and to have the ability to hold so troubled and invaded a land together for the boy king, John's son Henry III.

I have not yet spoken about the manner of King John's death, or the events that preceded it. My mind runs on in its own way, back and forth, remembering many things, while I sit looking out on the Thames and the swans, and Henry III's new abbey of Westminster.

6

As John himself was by far the youngest of Henry II's sons by Eleanor, having been conceived in a belated attempt at reconciliation, the men about him were mostly new and did not remember the old king's ways. William the Marshal was the exception, who had moreover been faithful to Henry throughout his wars with his sons, even on one occasion unhorsing Richard Coeur de Lion in hot pursuit. However in my early years at court, the Marshal was for the most part in Ireland. His life was a legend even I cannot query, but all I knew meantime was that he came home at the king's death to rule England as justiciar for the young Henry III, a thin pious child with his mother's golden hair. William the Marshal saw to it that there was no unrest after the succession of a minor, and in the three years that remained to him governed strongly even at his great age. The man who was to become my husband succeeded him at his death in 1219. Three years later, we were married; which in itself is proof that Hubert had shown enough ability, and had gained enough respect at home and abroad, to aspire to the hand of a princess, even one no longer young. Of all that I will speak soon, but meantime want to remember the loyal men.

Fair Rosamund's sons were among them. The elder, Geoffrey, who had been with his father at Chinon, was by now archbishop of York, and a pleasanter one than Roger of old. The younger son, William earl of Salisbury, had what must have been his mother's features and grace of long limbs; certainly he had no resemblance to old Henry II, downright and lacking in grace as he had been, they say, though with charm for women. Salisbury's looting of the French ships at Damme I have related, and shortly, when the young king's still younger brother, Richard, was sixteen, he rode with the boy to save Gascony for England. That had been Queen Eleanor's old inheritance, or part of it, with a new name, and the home of very good wine. Later it was lost for other reasons.

Henry II himself would never have lost anything, at least while he was in health; by unremitting energy and foresight he had in some way contrived to keep the enormous Angevin empire together, ranging as it did from Toulouse to, in his view, Scotland. Henry's son King John, although he fought hard in vain to keep Normandy, in fact concerned himself less with the lands across the Channel than with his English kingdom; I think he loved England. He travelled constantly up and down as I say, knowing every road and obscure way to the north parts; and everywhere, as I have also said, he saw to the needs of the poor, who were never despised by him or sent away unheard. The keeping of laws he ensured, also the collection of scutage, which is one more reason for the barons' resentment; being bereft of money hurt them, and they had been used to do as they would in such matters and in others. A small core recognized the need for strong rule by a king who liked to see things for himself; but in general this was the real core of later events at Runnymede, where King John was forced to sign a charter which not only enraged him – he had his father's temper – but which the pope, whose obedient son John now outwardly was, shortly declared null and void.

Court itself was a decorous place, with the king often away, and the young queen presiding at Woodstock or Windsor in seemly enough fashion. I and my sisters stayed near her and knew little except what we saw. What news I received was mostly by way of my uncle David of Huntingdon, when he came to court, or now and again from Alexander concerning Scotland.

David my uncle had been long ago in the East, in Constantinople on the way to the Holy Land, and had heard the jabber of Greek in the streets and picked up a little. As well as the hair-splitting theologians who surrounded the emperor he met others, monks from the monasteries, who had garnered certain ancient wisdom from long before the coming of Christ or of Imperial Rome. He used to rejoice in the tales of Homer and the lascivious early gods, and now we were grown almost beyond marriage would tempt us with them, his handsome face impassive and a twinkle in his eye. One tale I recall, and which made me think of King John and

Queen Isabelle, was of the god Poseidon, who fancied a wavelet named Amphitrite and had her pursued by a dolphin to far parts till she was brought unwillingly to him, though, as my uncle remarked, any nearer wavelet would have done as well. Amphitrite bore her husband a great many children and continued to loathe him. It became evident as soon as King John was dead which way the land lay, because Isabelle made haste to wed the man to whom she had been betrothed when John first laid eyes on her in France, and she bore Hugh de la Marche thereafter a great many children as well. These Poitevins, as they were later known, invaded England like a swarm of locusts in the next reign, as if to avenge themselves for the treatment of their sire when John had reft his child-bride from him. Hugh himself had been chained in an ox-cart and conveyed from France to Corfe, with twenty-four followers whom John is said separately to have starved to death in Bristol castle. They had all of them helped Arthur of Brittany in his brief war for his rights, when old Queen Eleanor, the royal grandmother, was besieged by her grandson at Mirebeau and John her son came swiftly with an army to rescue her. He was a better soldier than many gave him credit for; it is doubtful if even his brother Richard Coeur-de-Lion could long have held the Angevin empire their father had maintained.

    I thought of all that, and of how John himself resembled a little cock-sparrow, stout now and bejewelled beneath his white hair. Perhaps he inherited the love of splendour from his mother; at Eleanor's coronation she had worn, they tell me, her rich hair wound in plaits round and round her head, and the plaits themselves were studded with gems. The Abbey then had been filled with purple silks and gleaming brocades in the manner of Constantinople, where Eleanor had travelled with her first husband Louis VII. By my time, things were plainer.

They told many false stories about King John. When he journeyed through the Isle of Wight it was said he burned down, each morning, the house which had sheltered him the night before. I do not believe this any more than I believe the tale of the poisoned egg sent to Matilda Fitzwalter because she would not lie with him. Certainly John was lustful; he was also vengeful. The outspoken de Braose woman died most dreadfully, but she had made an untoward remark in public about the murder of Arthur of Brittany. I used to hear the lowing of the splendid herd of white cattle she had sent, in hoped-for propitiation, as a gift to the queen. They had red ears. It is a breed long known in Galloway, but in England was considered a marvel, especially the bull.

Despite all this I was sad when I heard of the death of the king, of a fever at Newark, where he had been carried in a litter. I think rage at several recent events, Runnymede among others, had perhaps brought on the fever; also the late disaster when all the baggage-carts containing, among other things, the regalia, were swamped and lost in a sudden Norfolk tide.

However they had to circulate unkind stories after the king

was dead, saying he had died of a surfeit of peaches and cider like old Henry I Beauclerc with his famous ultimate feast of lampreys. Also, John having asked to be buried at Worcester near the shrine of St Wulfstan, this was done; but a tale grew to the effect that the abbot, at his prayers in the cathedral by night, had heard a voice from the tomb crying to be rid of the souls of all those John had murdered, who were tormenting him; and to have his body taken out of so holy a place and buried nameless in a nearby field, which was done, and thereafter no crops would grow there. This is one more story I do not believe.

In whatever way it had all happened, the news of King John's death was no doubt welcome to my unforgiven kinsman the sixth earl of Warren and Surrey. He made haste to kneel before the new child king, and was thereafter so much about Henry III that he soon once more earned his name of Cognatus Regis; young Henry was easily influenced, and his mother was by then abroad with her new husband. The Marshal meantime was father and mother to the crowned boy, and at court and, rising by means of quiet industry and his reputation for having saved Dover in the French invasion, was Hubert, Hadwisa's widower; she died the year after her former husband John.

Henry III was king of England, therefore, at nine years old. They crowned him, as his father's crown was lost in the eternal waters, with a gold circlet Queen Isabelle used to wear round her neck and lent for the occasion. This was not even at

Westminster, but at Gloucester, where the royal family had taken refuge in what were still widespread disturbances. When the Marshal came home they ceased. As for the French prince Louis, we heard no more of his claim to England through his strong-minded wife Blanche; he was king of France, and she its queen, within seven years. By that time, I was a wife.

7

Alexander's coronation at Scone in 1214 must have been a magnificent affair, with the great sapphire he had himself bought from the Hansa of Berwick set in the crown, which was new, having been made for the first time for Malcolm IV in 1153. The Maiden's mother, my grandmother Ada de Warenne, who would then act as regent for the twelve-year-old boy till he was older, had witnessed Stephen's coronation in England, which gave him the advantage over King Henry Beauclerc's daughter Matilda, rightful heiress but not yet crowned. Hitherto the Scots kings had only thought it needful to be anointed on the sacred Stone of Scone. Countess Ada introduced coronation as well as anointing. There were still rivals who would cause trouble if there was the least doubt about her son's rights, and the shining sight of young Malcolm in his crown and robes would impress the watching people, while as always a seannachie recited, in sing-song Gaelic, all the king's ancestry back to misty Scota, who was said to have brought the Stone from Egypt. Before that it had been Jacob's pillow when he had the dream of angels ascending and descending a ladder that reached to heaven. I have never understood why God favoured the wily Jacob rather than his brother Esau, who had a forgiving nature in the end; but there it was. I only regret that I could not be present to see the Maiden's crown set on Alexander's red head, and watch him show himself to the people.

He made a strong king, young and still unmarried. They were friendly days then with England, and we, his sisters, were treated less as hostages than as guests. King John liked to have the sons and daughters of his nobility sent to him at court, as I have said, partly no doubt in order that their parents might obey him, but also because he liked young company. It was in any case a tradition with Scottish royalty; the Lion's brother, my uncle David of Huntingdon, had lived at the English court half his boyhood, and old King David all of it. We three sisters – Marjory stayed on – learned the precise courtly dances as I had told Alexander we would; heard lays from the time of Queen Eleanor, who had been a lover of troubadours' songs, rightly since one such lay had rescued, in the end, Coeur-de-Lion; being sung below his Austrian prison, so that he sang back. We attended mass, now the interdict was over, in abbeys and cathedrals less glorious than King David's nine great foundations in Scotland, or the new Lantern of the North Alexander had started to build at Elgin when he had leisure between rebels in Galloway and the Isles. My grandmother's, begun at Haddington, called the Lamp of Lothian, was also still building, though she herself was dead near forty years.

Thereafter King John was less friendly, partly by reason of the coming of Prince Louis, and after that I think he merely kept a grudge against my brother about Tweed ports. After he died the wise Marshal improved matters, and after the Marshal's death it was arranged that Alexander II of Scots should marry Joan of England, one of John's daughters by his queen Isabelle.

I had never seen Joan, who had been brought up in the charge of the man she was expected to marry, Hugh de la Marche. However her mother hastened overseas after King John's death and married him instead, this being a reunion of the couple betrothed in childhood. Isabelle tried to pretend that she had made the marriage to safeguard the interests of her son Henry III, but nobody believed her. They were no doubt happy enough, but Joan was probably in the way, and it was convenient to dangle her as a bride before my brother, who had never seen her. Nor, as I say, had I.

The marriage was to be at York, which had for long been a meeting-place between north and south. I will describe Joan briefly; she appeared miserable, resentful and plain, and I never in all my life saw her smile. Nevertheless I recall that place, and time, joyfully. It was there, at the very same hour in York Minster, that I married Hubert de Burgh, justiciar of England. That was in 1221. Before that, perhaps the most notable happening of John's reign had taken place at Runnymede.

8

Queen Isabelle seemed to have accepted her earlier fate, and had borne King John a handsome brood of children by 1215. Of these the heir, young Henry, was perhaps the least attractive despite his golden hair. He had a sly uncertain way with him, and a strangely drooping left eyelid. He did not agree well with his younger brother Richard, even when they were small. I liked Richard best of all the royal children; he reminded me of Alexander, being frank and manly even at six years old. He and his witty sister Isabella were allies from the beginning. The queen cared little for any of them. She remained quiet, correct and passive, and whether the tale of the hanged lover was true, or general confusion with the hanging by Llewelyn, long ago in Wales, of his wife's de Braose lover, I know not. A de Braose certainly haunted Windsor, the skeletal ghost who had, they say, gnawed at her dead son's flesh at last in an attempt to stay alive, while the gift of white cattle lowed outside her cell.

Despite all this we women kept to our usual avocations,

and let great events proceed as they would. However recalling the fate of Matilda de Braose made one remember that down in the field, that day, among the myriad tents, Archbishop Langton would set his name first of all to a charter which at least promised hearing of one's crime before being held unendingly in prison. I was playing chess with Isabel, and Marjory looked idly out of the window to tell us of the arrival of the pope's legate, and young Richard and Isabella stared over our shoulders at the game, and with them were William Bardolf and little John de Burgh. All of them stared fascinated at the board with its carved kings and queens and bishops and castles, as grand in their way as the parley below.

'Castles are straight, bishops are crooked,' said Isabella, and everyone burst out laughing, for by now there were clustered mitres down in the field, the assembled prelates trying to keep their vestments from being stained by the waterlogged ground without losing dignity. There was much ceremony thereafter, and we went on with our game of chess. Young Isabella continued to make pert remarks, for she was already considered witty, and for a child to be told so is bad for it. It was particularly hard on Isabella, who later on married the emperor and disappeared into his harem, taking with her the magnificent baggage-train from England which included cooking-pots of solid silver. All that was still in the future, that day at Runnymede.

'They say the king is writhing with rage on the ground in his tent,' remarked William Bardolf, having gone to the door.

This was nothing new; the Plantagenet temper manifested itself in such ways often, and Henry II had once torn his clothes and chewed the floor-straw as well at mere mention of my father, in Normandy.

I moved a knight absently, thereby losing the game in the end, but I was thinking how the boy Bardolf was Beatrice de Warenne's, the sixth earl's cousin's, son by her first marriage, whereas her second husband, whom I had not then met, was a man who had risen from nothing and who was named now as probable justiciar soon; young John's father, Hubert de Burgh. I heard the name murmured amid the sound, at last, of the departing multitudes after the signing of Magna Carta.

Hubert was to remain justiciar for seventeen years, and for most of these was almost king himself. It is time I said more about him; he is so constantly in my memory and my prayers that I tend to dwell openly on other events, as it were, keeping Hubert to myself.

The deep sound of the passing-bell sounded through England for my uncle David of Huntingdon in 1219. He had lived like the prince he was, and many legends died with him. We would miss his hospitality greatly, as his heir, still young, showed signs of being somewhat odd. He was to become known as John the Scot, and was a poor guerdon for Scotland. It is some years now since I heard that he had died after a fall from his horse; it is said that his wife had seen to it by poisoning him before he set out. His sisters were pleasanter, and inherited what was left; by then, things had changed with regard to Huntingdon.

After our uncle's death I and my sisters tended increasingly to accept the hospitality of the sixth earl Warren in the east of England. I had a certain sympathy with his first wife and an amused tolerance of the second. Before then, it is probable that he had an eye on one or other of us Scots princesses after he was returned to favour by the death of King John. The latter monarch had never forgiven him for cleaving to Prince Louis; almost the only instance when Cognatus Regis mistook his upward path. However he found it again in the new reign, and thereafter kept to prescribed ways. It was through him that I became acquainted with Hubert.

9

It was inevitable that Hubert and I should meet, and when we did so it was after the king's death and still in the brief remaining lifetime of poor Hadwisa. As I say I never saw her, though at the time she was not far off, we were in Lincolnshire and I and my sisters were guests, for the time, of the newly forgiven Cognatus Regis, who had made haste to bow the knee to little Henry III and had beguiled him with smiles, flaunting fesse-checky banners and rich presents. The last were not quite on the level of poor Matilda de Braose's milk-white cattle with red ears, but gifts enough to fascinate a boy. There was no doubt that the sixth earl had charm, but it was always used for a purpose. When he sent, by a messenger in a tabard, our invitation to Grantham, which he had lately acquired, I knew it was for the possibility of assessing which one of us should be his next bride. His countess was far from well, and had not yet done her duty.

We paused on the way to rest at my uncle David's, who was still alive but complaining about his bones; then travelled on with small gear. The poor countess welcomed us timidly and had us shown at once to our chamber. Later Cognatus – he had not yet fully acquired the title, but so I always think of him – came, bowing assiduously, plying us with wine, and having a good look, especially at Isabel; it was evident I would not do unless something happened to Alexander, in which case Cognatus might become king of Scots. As for Marjory, her lovely bones were as slender as a bird's, so breeding prospects were doubtful in the eyes of a possible bridegroom by now somewhat desperate as regards that. Isabel and I laughed about him afterwards in bed. During the days that followed, he made so much of us both that by the end I said to Isabel that I would ride out alone and leave her to deal with his sheep's eyes by herself. She could scarcely contain her mirth when I rode off on a borrowed palfrey from the stables, setting my heels in hard. After so much pomp and attention, I needed solitude.

I rode on eastwards by the sun, not knowing where I was going except that there seemed small danger in the flat open countryside. I was plainly dressed and no target for thieves, and rode swiftly. The land was flooded with many islands, from some of which house-smoke rose. At last I came to what seemed like a great sea, and knew this must be The Wash, which had swallowed up poor King John's treasure shortly before he died. Many had searched for it in vain, and legends had grown about what lay deep in the hungry sands at the mouth of the treacherous river opening there; what was lost was said to have included the imperial crown with which the empress Matilda, John's grandmother, had been crowned in course of her first marriage. I have that sour variety of mind that spoils legends, and I happened to know, and have stated already, that Matilda, King Henry Beauclerc's daughter, had never been crowned, either as empress or as Lady of England, which was the nearest she achieved to being queen. However it was not a subject to be mentioned at court, even now; her son Henry II had in the end succeeded.

I had been staring out at the grey eternal water and reflecting on such things, and on my life, and the lives of all of us, and of what was to happen next if anything did; and became aware that I was not alone, that a man of middle height, in a dark hood and tunic, had come up silently behind me, having already dismounted from his horse. Its hooves had made no sound on the boggy turf and I had not heard him come. I had an instant's fear that he might be a robber; then at sight of his face, knew that he was none.

How can I say clearly that within instants, we both knew a chiming of our fates, that we would meet again, that this moment was to be the first of many, the beginning of all things for us together? I cannot remember what our first exchanged word was, and it does not matter; I think Hubert, having said who he was, pointed out the names of the sandbanks and the deeps, and that I should not be riding here alone. 'The ground can give way without warning,' he said. 'You must permit me to escort you back to the solid road.' He added that he knew these parts, having been born here. 'It wasn't yesterday,' he said, looking at me. He must have been over forty then; it did not matter, I myself was no longer a young woman. As I say, we knew already that our ways would cross again. I recall saying I had met his little son John at Windsor that time we had all looked out on the famous field that is called Runnymede, where, among other happenings, Hubert had been made justiciar.

I learned more about him after that; the thin wild creature who had been Hadwisa of Gloucester was either newly dead or about to die when we met, and, as he did all things, Hubert mourned her correctly though she had never been a wife to him in fact. They lie who say he seduced me into marriage with an eye to the crown of Scotland; we were married in York four years after as I have said, alongside my brother Alexander, king of Scots, and King John's daughter Joan, who at her age could have been expected to produce heirs and rule me out of the succession. Nobody could have foreseen that she would not, or that Alexander my brother would have to wait for her death sixteen years after to marry again, a noble French lady, and get himself a son.

It turned out, instead, that I was the one who was fertile even yet; and after Meggotta's birth my husband's enemies began to work against him with the king, who by then was no longer a child.

10

The murmuring that Hubert was not of high birth no doubt began when he replaced the great Marshal at the latter's death in 1219. However there was nobody else fit to occupy the place of justiciar, and a boy of twelve, as Henry III was by then, was by no means yet fit to reign. Hubert de Burgh was known to be a man of sense, probity and courage. Also, the young king at that time liked him greatly, perhaps because young John de Burgh was already familiar about court.

Hubert understood the king as he understood his son and stepson. A boy of twelve needs different treatment from a boy of nine, as Henry III had been at his father's death. Then, in bewilderment, he had suffered his mother's gold collar to be placed on his head for a crown. Now, there were discussions about a grander one, to be fashioned and worn on great occasions such as a second coronation at Westminster in what was still the Confessor's old Abbey, completed in Hastings year. I was called in for advice, as I could tell the boy Henry about my father the Lion's crown, by now Alexander's, and made more glorious than ever with the great sapphire in front. 'It may have come from Kashmir,' I said. 'That jewel is known for its healing, and in the east is only worn by kings.'

Henry's drooping left eyelid raised itself to reveal a certain gleam of interest; and I went on to tell him about the first Scots coronation, that of Malcolm the Maiden, and the sacred Stone that had once been Jacob's pillow, from which that doubtful character watched the ascending and descending of the angels of God before moving on.

'A crown was new for us in Scotland then,' I said. 'You in England have worn one time out of mind.' I am not certain, in fact, when crowns came to England; it used to be several kingdoms, as in the north.

'My father's is lost,' the boy said sadly, still recalling the disaster at Swinshead three years since; he knew no efforts to recover the drowned treasure had succeeded. 'But your throne, sire, is not,' put in Hubert quickly. As often, this quickness, which was Henry's also, warmed the young king at a time when boys are uncertain if things change. Henry III was already suspicious by nature; lacking his mother, far off in Lusignan with her new husband, lacking the Marshal who for three years had been his rock, unable to agree in anything with his younger brother Richard, who had a better head than he, the king of England felt solitary and unsure of himself. We continued, therefore, to discuss crowns, their forms and patterns, for the boy had a sense of beauty. We agreed that the old Confessor's crown, judging by his seal, seemed to be nothing but a lumpish gold wreath; yet on the great tapestry ordered by Bishop Odo it is shown as made of trefoils, to signify the Trinity. 'I should like that,' said Henry. 'I'd like to rebuild the abbey as well, in a year or two. It's very old now.' Some time about then he laid a stone for the Lady Chapel, which led to many things.

Nobody mentioned the king of France's crown, with its lily forms. The justiciar and I smiled at one another as he escorted me on his arm from the royal presence; we were equal in height. We talked seldom, as those feel they do who know already that they see eye to eye.

Hubert spoke now, at the door. 'You are a stranger here, as I am,' he said in a low voice. 'Is it possible that a princess and the son of a humble knight may console one another?'

It took a little while to arrange our marriage. My brother the king in Scotland had to be formally consulted; but Alexander knew that I would not agree to any union I disliked. There were of course many at court who resented the betrothal of a man they called an upstart to one of the royal blood of both Scotland and England through Margaret Atheling, but the king's mind was with us after the talk of crowns and sapphires. Despite the inevitable rumour that Hubert had seduced me, it was all arranged within two years, as the returned princess Joan would conveniently make a bride for Alexander. As early as 1217 he had made peace after the former alliance with Louis, so that there was agreement between our countries for the time.

11

There is an old English word *burh*, no doubt from when the Danes began to settle in East Anglia. First it meant a place, then later a town when these arose. My husband's family may have been part Danish from the old settlers; but Hubert's steady and industrious mind was Saxon. He was the younger son of a small Norfolk landowner and had to make his way in the world. One of his brothers had entered the Church, which is a sure way to promotion, but Hubert had no such calling. If he has been blamed for making ambitious marriages, this was one other way; and in addition to that he was good to his wives and did not live on their dowries, but served his country manfully as long as he was let.

My kinsman the sixth earl had lands in Norfolk, and was Hubert's patron. Apart from the first marriage to a girl from the Isle of Wight – she died soon – the earl encouraged Hubert to marry his own widowed second cousin, formerly Beatrice de Warenne, who already had the son by her first marriage I have mentioned, William Bardolf. My husband by then having won respect for his long defence of Dover Castle against the French, Beatrice married him without too much condescension. I became very fond of their son John, not only because he was Hubert's son but for himself. He is not, by now, too pleased with me.

When Beatrice died the marriage to Hadwisa of Gloucester took place, and although as stated it kept Hubert firmly in high places it was one of compassion only. He saw the poor creature nursed till she died, and in the meantime went on with his life and study, which had included much law.

To return to the de Warenne earls, with whom I am connected by way of my grandmother Countess Ada, the marriages of the sixth followed each other in due course, with pomp and prosperity. The first Albini bride, though royally connected, was a disappointment, but the second called herself Marshaless of England, a sign of the esteem in which her father William the Marshal had been held, also her brothers, by then mostly dead with violence. Maud Marshal already had sons by her first spouse, Hugh Bigod, the earl of Norfolk, or so he claimed; that family is shifty. King Stephen, in his muddle-headed and good-natured fashion, had given the same titles to de Bigods and de Warennes both, no doubt in the hope of pleasing either side, which did not happen. The new marriage of a Bigod widow to the sixth earl of Warren and Surrey settled that ancient matter, and Maud the Marshaless at last bore my kinsman his heir some years after my own marriage and the birth of my little daughter. Not long after, the Marshaless died, no doubt the births of her eleven children all told having been too much for her constitution. I attended her heart-burial at Lewes, but will speak of that in its place.

The changing of Cognatus' name back to his mother's from Plantagenet meant with truth that the de Warennes were there first. The original earl had been a friend and fighter for William of Normandy long before Hastings, and as a reward had been married early to the Norman duke's oldest daughter, got before papal permission arrived for Duke William's own marriage to be ratified at Rome. William and his bride Matilda of Flanders were too much in love to wait, and later built two abbeys in penance at Caen by papal request, being thereafter recognised as man and wife. King Henry Beauclerc, born in England, was their last child of ten; Gundreda was their first, and Henry I exhibited that jealousy towards her which he showed to most of his kin, even to the murder of Rufus and the long, imprisonment of Curthose, who had a better right to the crown than he.

No doubt it was a punishment of God that Beauclerc's heir was drowned, leaving most of the king's twenty-one illegitimate children alive, including Robert of Gloucester. The civil wars between the late Henry I's daughter Matilda and King Stephen her cousin followed, as all know, and ended with the coming of the Plantagenets in Henry II, Matilda's son. My cousin the sixth earl remained well aware that his mother, Countess Isabel, the first de Warenne's great-granddaughter, who had been married to the Angevin king's bastard half-brother, had a far older name than the kings of England themselves, He continued nevertheless to cultivate their company.

I am glad that I was not like Countess Isabel, forced to take a husband by reason of great lands. I brought little to Hubert that day in York, 1221, except great love. We were both of us people of few words, and said little of it; but there it was. Like my late uncle David, I had waited to marry as I chose; he would not, like my father the Lion, take a bride at last at the bidding of Henry II, but waited till he could decide for himself.

The double wedding was seemly, but not extravagant: Hubert was anxious to garner money for the king. I embraced Alexander, not seen for nine years and a month. There were joy-bells, wine and feasting, and the folk of York crowded to see the dependable red-haired figure of the king of Scots, aged twenty-three, and his English bride. Joan and I were like dun sparrows by comparison with Marjory, who was my attendant; Isabel had a cold and stayed in bed. Marjory was so radiant with beauty I cannot describe it, and Henry Ill, aged fourteen, gazed at her in church and afterwards with the awe of a child who looks upon an angel or a jewel, and cannot believe his eyes.

The English king had of course seen Marjory before, more than once; but perhaps the splendour of York Minster had rendered him amenable. He certainly fell in love with my sister then and remained so many years. It was not however thought politic to have further ties with Scotland which would prevent Henry's being available to a foreign alliance through marriage. He took a long time over that, and changed his mind so often that he became known as a perjurer or else odd, especially after the later business of the unfortunate princess from Ponthieu.

Nevertheless Henry was no oddity, being full man; unlike his father he was chaste, and took no mistresses, but waited for a wife till he was twenty-eight, and thereafter was faithful.

I cannot say I concerned myself too greatly with Henry's fate, as to have my hand firmly clasped in a certain quiet man's own was enough for me, and to feel the rings, one silver and one gold, sliding on my finger and on his, beneath the silk cloth before the great altar.

Later, Isabel, when she had recovered, asked me how Hubert and I had fared in bed. All I could say then, or can say now, is that it is a most commendable thing for a spinster to bed with a widower. I did not tell her what Hubert said to me at last, as we lay together, man and wife.

'To feel my heart beat against yours means more to me than all England.' That, if they had known, was an answer to his enemies.

My sister knew, of that, no more than I had said until she herself married, later on, Roger Bigod of Norfolk, a match arranged by the sixth earl with the kin of his Marshaless. By that time it was no longer considered advisable to have ties with Scotland other than those which still, though frail, existed.

As for Marjory, she waited, as had the Mother of God, like the king knowing no carnal union, yet not a nun, as she had no vocation. It was many years before she was permitted to wed the earl of Pembroke, and like Isabel she had no children. The delay was because of my position and Meggotta's, held by us as long as Alexander continued without heirs, as in direct line for the crown of Scotland. It was not until Marjory was considered past childbearing that she was able to marry, and then the marriage was cut short by tragedy. Of all our fates, mine was the most fortunate; I knew it at the time and have known it since, whatever else has befallen.

How can I describe contentment? I had thirteen years of it with Hubert my husband. From the day of our marriage that time in York, we were one mind and one flesh. It is true what Christ said concerning marriage. It is moreover pleasant beyond words for a woman to feel herself, for the first time, cherished. From my birth and childhood in Scotland I had been somewhat unwelcome till the heir was born, although my mother loved me out of duty, as she loved everyone. The Lion grew to be fond of me, as he was of all his children by different mothers, and by the end, as I grew to a kind of wisdom, to trust me as he had done that day at Dunfermline. However I had never before been loved totally, for myself, or because I was myself and none other, my every wish foreseen and met, all burdens taken from me, all decisions made with my agreement as far as it was possible in the high position Hubert held. All wives are not used so.

It had seemed to me certain that this calm and confident Norfolk man would take good care of me and of England, and so he did as long as he was let. Over the years, especially after our daughter's safe birth, I dare say I grew complacent; certain that nothing could destroy our happy and comfortable life till it wound by nature to its end.

I was wrong. That is well seen now, as I look back. In the matter of Meggotta's marriage I caused harm to her and to her father. I acted for the best, but to this day I blame myself bitterly. It is useless to do so, after all, or to repine. In an old age I should soon reach perhaps I may be the better able to recall, instead, the early years of my marriage, our joy at the coming and birth of our child, the pleasure it gave us to have the wardship soon of little Richard de Clare. I will make myself forget the jealous talk and scandal, the scrambling for high places to oust my husband, the gradual change in the king. Perhaps it will not be hard to discipline myself to remember joy, and to prepare for it again after my death.

II

1

Hubert had three castles in Gwent. Like most households we moved about from one to the next with our gear, our little child, her nurse, and Hubert's retainers, often also at first the king and his. Later there were other castles in Carmarthen and Cardigan, and the Marcher lands. All of it was no doubt to keep an eye on the doings of Llewelyn ap Iowerth, prince of Wales, the impressive figure who had come long ago to Norham on the Tweed. I asked my husband what harm there would be in letting Llewelyn govern his own principality in peace, as he seemed well able to do. He would be unlikely, if so, to trouble England.

'You are on his side, being a Scot,' Hubert replied. This was true, although I am part Norman, the Celtic blood in ancient times was the same; also, I recalled hearing of the death of my young uncle Malcolm IV after the Welsh campaigns of Henry II, which had had to be abandoned by reason of the terrain. That was unaltered.

Nevertheless I knew Hubert had at all costs to defend young Henry III's interests and be watchful as the dead Marshal had been, that England might not be nibbled away at the edges. King Henry had relied on the Marshal as a father, but by now he himself was no longer a child. He had flashes of independence with which my husband knew how to deal if left to do so; yet Henry was obsessed by the knowledge that Philip Augustus of France had declared himself of age at fourteen and had then reigned fully, using his personal seal.

Hubert told him the circumstances were different. Philip Augustus had succeeded a father who had lain speechless, paralysed and unable to reign, but still remained king, for a year before his death. 'England is still restless after Runnymede,' Hubert told John's son. 'Some of your lords are on one side, some on the other. It would be disastrous if the country lacked a strong rule for the next few years, till your manhood, my liege.'

He did not add that Philip Augustus of France had been born with a wise head on his shoulders, whereas Henry III had an uncertain and peevish temper from the beginning. This had to be allowed for if he was not to take permanent offence; sometimes there were near-scenes. Hubert would then defer to the king, or appear to, then later on set matters in train as he had at first intended.

Being a Plantagenet, Henry was also spoiling for war of some kind as soon as possible. It was found in the instance of a knight named Fawkes de Bréauté. I had known Fawkes somewhat about court. He was a braggart of a fellow, full of himself in the way men later said my husband had been; but Hubert never made as much clamour. De Bréauté had the support of certain men who resented my husband, including loyal but stubborn old Ranulf of Chester, father-in-law to my late uncle David and not always aware of his own best interests. He made a notable disturbance at Christmas at Winchester, where we all kept the feast among wall-paintings and high masses, with the strong good presence of Stephen Langton, by now secure in his see of Canterbury and present for a part of the festival. Nevertheless there was talk even there of a man who had cried out lately in London 'God and our lord Louis be our aid' after all this time. Matters were not yet peaceful.

De Bréauté had made a powerful marriage, but was not on terms with his wife. He was asked to surrender, as part of my husband's policy, certain castles. He refused to hand over Plympton in Devon, saying he held it in his wife's right. As for Bedford, he held unreasonably on. Sixteen actions were brought against him for various misdeeds, and his brother William seized one of the judges and carried the poor man, bound, into the castle. By this time, denied domestic comfort and finding opposition on all sides, Fawkes was breathing fire and calling every man in England a traitor, swearing that he would make war. 'The realm will be too small to hold them,' he shouted at my husband. Hubert did not reply, and to my relief I was not present at the final affray.

Fawkes declined to appear to answer a formal accusation of felony made direct to the king, and was therefore declared outlaw. After a further refusal Henry and my husband moved to Bedford castle and laid siege, with the unfortunate judge still inside. Young King Henry was unfeignedly delighted; it was his first taste of war.

William, Fawkes's brother, refused to admit the king. He called from the battlements that Fawkes was exempt from prosecution as he had taken a vow to go to the Holy Land. It is regrettable that that excuse has become mundane. The archbishop, his vizor still down, promptly excommunicated Fawkes, which renders the vow null.

Bedford was besieged for eight weeks, with knight-service and levies undertaken by the bishops. There was however plenty of food inside the castle, and the late King John had strengthened it notably. While Henry raged outside, enjoying his rage, two men of import came. One was old Ranulf. The other was Peter des Roches the Poitevin, whom it still hurts me to remember as bishop of Winchester; evil should not as readily enter the house of God. Ranulf in hope tried to mend matters; Fawkes must go, he said, to his friend Llewelyn of Wales to put everything on a proper footing.

I believe Fawkes did try to see Llewelyn, but was not welcomed. He set spurs to his horse once more, and returned to ask for a respite while his case was considered at Rome. This request was denied.

Meantime the outer works fell, to the excitement of the young king, and the inner keep was then set on fire to drive the besieged out. Next day they were absolved, made their confessions and, by the king's order, were hanged. Henry had sworn that this should happen, and as we were later to learn, he would never forswear an oath. However three knights were cut down halfway. and caused instead to join the Knights Templars for service at Jerusalem; a hard life and a celibate one. I said to Hubert afterwards that they would be better dead.

'The king says he does not intend to allow evil customs,' Hubert replied wryly.

Fawkes, in tears – his wife had meantime thrown him out – arrived to the sight of his friends' limp bodies. He cast himself at the king's feet and was not despatched to join them, but ordered to leave England. A rascal had escaped and honest men were punished; it turned out later on that Fawkes had lied about the amount of money he was able to hand over. He told the king he had but forty shillings, yet years later, on his deathbed in far parts, he admitted that forty thousand marks had been deposited by him with the Templars. He had been sheriff of seven shires, and ended as nobody.

The main irritation for my husband during all this was that urgent business regarding Ireland and France had to be set aside to indulge a boy's spiteful whim. Later it appeared that the pope, who was hardly our neighbour, blamed the archbishop for bungling matters. Meantime Hubert appeared victorious, but the whole episode was quoted later on as one example of his arrogance. Moreover the difference between Peter des Roches of Winchester, and Stephen Langton the primate, flared into open dislike, formented by the de Bréauté matter. It remained unforgotten, and the great archbishop only had five years left to live. Had Langton been spared, all of our lives might have been different.

2

I came to know the great churchman well in the seven years between my marriage and his death. He and Hubert consulted one another frequently. Stephen Langton was the most saintly man I ever encountered, though his modesty would not have permitted him to agree. He would describe Pope Innocent III to me with affection, and none of the bowing and scraping the likes of Des Roches of Winchester would have provided. He and the pope, Loratio de'i Conti then, had studied together as young men at the University of Paris. Langton retained a strong feeling for the impulsive yet determined pontiff, the greatest, he maintained, since Pope Hildebrand. I kept my silence, for Hildebrand could be harsh and, in my view, had wrongly promulgated celibacy for all churchmen. However Langton described Innocent's prominent eyes, high colour and firm jaw, and the presence which overawed all who encountered him.

'I was a cardinal in his household, and there was no question of his authority there,' the archbishop said. He himself had been consecrated and given the see of Canterbury at Viterbo as a distinct improvement on the royal candidates, but it was six years before King John would let him land in England. Like Becket in his time, Langton had taken refuge at Pontigny. The Norman kings had had continuous feuds with their prelates; in earlier days the Saxon rulers had not contemplated such a thing. Stigand, Anselm, Becket and now Langton had all had their troubles with the various monarchs and been driven overseas. Fortunately young Henry III looked like being an obedient son of the pope, perhaps not having been made aware of Langton's name, first of any, on the great roll that is called Magna Carta.

It is true that the present good for the greatest number was Stephen Langton's watchword, but in private moments he would receive illumination from the Holy Spirit which gave rise to marvellous prayers. I was to use them to comfort myself later on, in the dark days to come when Hubert was in prison, my daughter and I in sanctuary.

Langton nevertheless fell out with the pope in the end, having refused to publish the barons' excommunication sent by Innocent on King John's submission to himself when the charter was declared void. This is the high-handed behaviour of a leader who is too far from events to understand them. Langton won the argument in the end and was reinstated, but died in ten years. There are so many dead, and I have outlived most.

3

In my happiness with Hubert and our child, I neglected my sister Isabel somewhat, and I blame myself for what happened to her. Had I been there, had we been able to laugh together over things and folk as we had done in the days when the sixth earl had an eye to one or other of us, she would not have fallen victim to a scoundrel.

At that time, the prospects for all the Lion's daughters were bright. The king had continued in love with Marjory and it was known he would ask for her hand when he was of age. As Henry was hesitant this did not happen till he was twenty-four, but meantime the attachment was known. I was the wife of the most powerful man in the kingdom, Alexander's queen had produced no heir, and Isabel herself was ripe for marriage, in fact overripe; she had long resented her spinster's state. All of this was noted by a Bigod, of the first family of the sixth earl's Marshaless; he was in fact the son, got young, of the eldest of her sons, and Isabel could have been his mother. It was not difficult for a young man of address to ensnare her, left alone as she was except for Marjory, who was neither practical nor suspicious. I myself, on once seeing this same Bigod, had told them both not to trust a man with light eyelashes, never thinking it would happen.

We were in Wales when we learned that Bigod had persuaded Isabel to elope with him. They were married at Alnwick, he having made sure of her on the way. Had she not been besotted, it would have occurred to her that that place, near as it was to escape over the border to our brother if there was need, had been the scene of two betrayals already; old King Malcolm Ceann Mór had been treacherously murdered there, his heir Edward dying of wounds nearby a few days after; and just before our own time the Lion himself had been captured by the English at Alnwick, found taking his ease in a field at the raising of a mist by the newest English saint. Of all places it would bring ill luck; and this poor Isabel endured in full measure through the years that followed. When our fortunes fell with Hubert, her husband repudiated her, advancing the claim, which was absurd, that there was consanguinity. Isabel had in fact disappointed him by bearing no heir, but as he neglected her by then it was not surprising. That family, the Bigods, were always unreliable since the time of old Hugh, who started the civil war in England by announcing that King Henry Beauclerc, on his deathbed, had disinherited his daughter Matilda in favour of his nephew Stephen of Blois. It was later proved that Hugh Bigod had not even been present at the deathbed; and moreover changed sides soon and fought for Matilda against Stephen.

Isabel fought the decree, and Bigod was forced by the church to take her back again within six years. Her position had been rendered wretched, and remained so; but she had a fighting spirit. She sojourned in Bigod's house for a year or two, then, unable to endure the situation, retired into Gloucestershire, where she is still.

Marjory's story was different.

The king petitioned to be allowed to marry her at last in 1231, but was refused in council; relations with Scotland were not then at their best, and it was still thought a bride from overseas was to be preferred. Marjory never said what she felt about all this; if she had any ambition to become queen of England we were not aware of it. Within four years, at the time of the king's own marriage, she was united with one of the Marshal's sons, perhaps the pleasantest of the five; most had been valorous, some had been wise, but Gilbert was gentle and had been intended for the Church, in which he had even taken minor orders. For this reason he was sneered at as unfit for knightly exercises, and moreover was, like the king, uncertain in decision. He loved Marjory and they were happy together, but Gilbert kept a resolution in his mind that he must nevertheless take the cross and go to the Holy Land. He lost, and then again won, the favour of the king, and having won it lingered after all with Marjory in England; then being goaded into taking part in a tournament the king had forbidden, mounted an Italian horse. It happened at a place near Hertford, and although I was not there the tale was told me.

Gilbert exerted himself valiantly, while the crowd, egged on by certain lords, jeered at him for a weakling and a craven priest whose wife was barren. He spurred his Italian charger at that and pulled sharply, too much so, on the reins, both of which broke. They say they had been tampered with earlier. The horse tossed its head, causing Gilbert a violent blow on the chest; this killed him. The horse bolted, and Gilbert's eldest brother Richard, who was in the tourney also, half blind with dust and sweat and the weight of his helmet, fell from his saddle and was dragged along by the stirrup. He never recovered from the internal injuries this caused, and meantime he and the fourth brother, Walter, who was there likewise, made a sad procession back to London with the corpse of Marjory's husband. All this harm was caused by the Poitevins, the king's half-brothers, Queen Isabelle's second brood, who had come at Henry's invitation to England by then and were eating it up, making marriages for themselves with English heiresses and others for their sisters with English nobles. They were enemies of the Marshal brothers for standing out against them in council; at one point they had had the title of Marshal itself declared forfeit by the king, but only for the time. Henry III was like wax in the, hands of whomsoever, at the moment, was close to him; and naturally his half-brothers were so, or was it natural? He never agreed in all his life with his full brother, Richard of Cornwall.

Gilbert Marshal's brother Richard died in Ireland after being wounded in a fight with the same enemies, or their servants; he was recovering, and playing dice, when the surgeon, who had been bribed, came, as he said, to see the wounds, and put a burning rod deep in them. Richard Marshal died of the resulting fever. That was later. There was a fifth brother, Anselm, who was delicate and did not live long after, ending the famous line with its blood from Strongbow and the kings of Leinster. It is a sad story, but two of us, Marjory and myself, at least knew happiness in marriage.

4

Good men make enemies. My husband's quiet determination and the primate's far-seeing piety, and consideration of ordinary folk, alienated the high-born and, by nature, the evil. The pope, as I have said already, suffered the drawback of being not in England but in Rome, and could learn nothing at first hand. Conflicting reports reached him, some from Archbishop Langton and others from Peter of Winchester, who opposed my husband bitterly and was no friend to Langton either. Nevertheless the primacy of Canterbury itself bore great weight, since the body of St Thomas lay there. Just as France and Wales were giving trouble, the pope wrote a letter which, to anyone knowing young Henry and Peter des Roches, was unwise; it stated that 'the king despite his tender years was mature in character, enough to have his own seal.' Moreover Peter of Winchester and his supporters were given the disposal of lands and the task of remitting everything direct to the king. Ranulf of Chester was considered important enough to be written to separately. My husband, evidently, was not. The lowered vizor and determined behaviour of Archbishop Langton at Bedford had borne sour fruit.

However affairs in Wales for once saved the day. A campaign was launched in which Hubert and the king rode side by side again to the castle of Builth, held meantime by Reginald de Braose, kin to those hanged by Llewelyn and starved and exiled by King John. My husband and King Henry relieved the castle, this time without tormented hangings, and thereafter occupied Montgomery. Terms of peace were arranged in early October and the lordship passed from South Powys to the king. Over the next year or two a town, and a new strong castle, were to be built there.

This gain placated young Henry, for the time; he had to have some matter to occupy him. My husband was thereafter able to give open support to the archbishop so that they could face their enemies together. Every time a castle had to be surrendered an enemy was made. One in particular would revenge himself later; he was sheriff and castellan of Hereford and also had great holdings in Ludlow and Meath, that last being in Ireland. His name was de Lacy. There were feuds over there from the early time of King John, which the Marshal had held in check in his lifetime; and the Marshal's sons, all five, fell heir to hatreds, as I have shown.

In England, those barons who obeyed old Ranulf of Chester as though he were God continued to whisper against my husband as an upstart. They made a demonstration outside the Tower of London, which was in Hubert's charge and where we were then residing. No one takes that fortress except those in charge of it, but I stared at the wall decorations and hangings chosen by Henry I's Good Queen my great-great-aunt and now growing shabby, and heard the clamour below. I had Meggotta sent to me in case the noise frightened her, but she was calm.

There was also a stormy conference at Waltham, where Hubert stood up and pointed a finger at Peter of Winchester as the source of all the trouble. Langton, by then ill, pacified the meeting, but it was only a postponement. The end of everything was, of course, that Henry III, by now sixteen, was given his privy seal.

We all spent Christmas at Northampton. Four days later old Ranulf submitted under threat of excommunication. I do not think Christ intended His body and blood to be given or withheld for political reasons, but there it was. The archbishop then distributed castles fairly, being a fair-minded man. We went on with our lives as usual; or at least, so it seemed.

5

Meggotta's doting father had made her a gift of three great manors. While she was still very small we went down to reside in one of them, Portslade, nearby the sea on the Sussex coast. Pleased as I was by my daughter's gifts – they would make her a splendid marriage in time – I was perturbed by the fact that, because of Meggotta's royal blood through myself, it had been decided that she, not Hubert's son John, should inherit all at her father's death. Not only was I unwilling to think of that event, but it seemed to me hard on young John de Burgh to lose his expected inheritance because of my marriage.

'He must carve his own way, as I had to,' was all Hubert replied. I knew John's kinsman the sixth earl would no doubt help him to preferment in time because of his mother's de Warenne blood-tie, but I still felt some regret.

On the day of which I must speak, John had come down with us and the nurse and Meggotta, to watch the grey waves of the Channel hurl themselves inshore. It was pleasant to gather differently coloured pebbles and gleaming shells, away from the tideline. I made Meggotta hold a shell to her ear.

'Hear the sea,' I told her, but she had seen her father come, dropped the shell and ran to him. I saw his dark figure pick her up, and he came towards us carrying her, but staring ahead. I heard the sea make its constant crying, and thought how it separated us from Normandy, long lost by the king's father.

Hubert set Meggotta down and spoke to me in a low voice. 'I want you to kneel with me in vigil tonight in the chapel. It is for the soul of one dead these twenty years, and another after.'

He surveyed the sea still, his face grim. I did not ask more at the times he wore such an expression; we shared all things, but respected one another's privacy. That evening, having seen Meggotta put to bed, I went down to the chapel. My lord was there already, and had lighted two candles before which he knelt. Hubert was devout in his prayers, and I made as if to kneel a little behind. The altar was prepared for mass, the mass of the dead.

My husband rose on hearing me approach, and taking my hand bade me come and kneel beside him. We were alone in the chapel with the priest when he came in, ready vested. The mass began, and as the dead were not named openly I did not know for whom I prayed with Hubert, but did so with all my heart.

He told me, later. 'Twenty years ago I was in Rouen, and Falaise also, where your father was held earlier. I disobeyed certain orders sent by King John. They were to blind and geld a boy of sixteen, his nephew Arthur of Brittany, rightful heir to the throne of England. I had not the heart to do it, nor yet the courage to let young Arthur escape; he had made war on the king. All I did was to warn him that men would come for that purpose to where he was confined, and that he must cry aloud for help, which I would send as if I knew nothing of it. This happened, and the young duke's screams brought rescue in time, led by a man named De Braose. You know well what befell his wife for speaking out so that the world knew what truly befell Arthur of Brittany.'

'Arthur was murdered,' I said. 'I do not know the manner of it.'

'The king caused it to be spread abroad that his nephew had tried to escape at Rouen and had drowned in the moat. He did not. John came in person and took the boy, weak then from prison, by night to the coast. Near Cherbourg there is a place with steep rocks, and John dragged his nephew from the saddle some way and then cut his throat while Arthur was crying out for his life to be spared, promising to abandon all rights to England in exchange for it. The words were drowned in blood, and his uncle cast him into the sea. I can never hear the crying of the waves without thinking of Arthur's young flesh devoured by fishes, and his white bones growing green on the sea's bed. He was a most beautiful boy, with blue eyes and golden hair, and he trusted me.'

'You could have done no more,' I said. 'King John would have revenged himself on you as he did on the de Braose family.'

'Ay. After his wife's death, and his son's, at Windsor the father was driven abroad, and died a pilgrim. You may ask how I know about the boy's death. There was a man, a Breton, present with the party of riders, who bore witness to what had been done. His name was Pierre de Maulac. He had no reason to lie. The Bretons loved their little duke, as they had loved his mother Constance, and her husband Geoffrey, Henry II's son, governed them well enough, but died young. John was still younger, and knew it.'

'Constance was my niece,' I said. 'My father's sister Margaret married Conan of Brittany, then when he failed to rule she and Constance were taken to England by the old king, and kept there.' I recalled that Arthur's sister Eleanor, the Pearl of Brittany, was still held close prisoner in Gloucester castle, and would never be set free. The Bretons had waited long, and in the end had chosen a husband for the eldest daughter of Constance's second marriage to rule them.

'King John is dead,' I said. 'He will have paid for his crimes before God. Whose was the other name you remembered?'

'De Braose's. He did not deserve to suffer for his wife's tongue.'

'Well, you will not suffer from mine,' I said, to cheer him. As the sound of the sea saddened Hubert, we soon moved away from Portslade. There were other manors of Meggotta's, in Essex and Leicester.

It was two or three years after that visit that my husband was created earl of Kent. It seemed nothing could go amiss for us, despite the envious tongues.

*

It brought Meggotta great joy to have a playmate of exactly her own age. Richard de Clare, soon to be earl of Gloucester, became Hubert's ward during those years. He seemed a dear little boy, handsome and with a direct gaze, though close-mouthed. Naturally I thought of him at once as a husband for my child, whose own estates would be as great as his when she was grown. I do not think I am more of a matchmaker than most mothers; but seeing the pair play together contentedly, it seemed to me a better prospect than a cold arrangement to be made later on with some stranger of high degree.

The wardship itself had come indirectly to us through poor Hadwisa, who had been the youngest of three sisters. Nevertheless Henry II, on her betrothal to his favourite son John, saw to it that she, not they, inherited the great Gloucester appanages. When John later divorced Hadwisa, he kept her lands. Shortly he forced Geoffrey de Mandeville to marry her and pay the enormous sum I have spoken of for the rights to these. As it happened, both Geoffrey and Hadwisa died childless. The lands went back to her elder sister Amice, who had married Gilbert de Clare. That family had long held lands in Hertford, and my little Richard – so I thought of him – in the end fell heir to Gloucester and Hertford both.

He was a secretive child, who would hold on to any gift he received on his name-day, not sharing it, saying fiercely if asked, 'It's mine.' This I think was because of his mother's remarriage a year after his father's death abroad. Richard was old enough to remember the knight with three chevrons who had ridden off to Antwerp on the king's behalf, to meet the princes of the empire, and who did not return except as a corpse. Gilbert de Clare died in Brittany, and his body was solemnly conveyed to Plymouth by ship, then to Tewkesbury to be buried there. Richard knew little more till his mother married the king's brother, who became his stepfather and bore his name. For a child, this meant much uncertainty and change; for a long time Richard trusted nobody. I made Meggotta share her own sweetmeats and cherries with him, which she did gladly. By slow stages he learned to trust us, even when he heard of the death of his mother in childbed, yellow with jaundice. It was, by then, no doubt like hearing of the death of a stranger. He clung to us, Meggotta and myself, then. That he remained undisturbed in sanctuary with us meant that he had been forgotten in the press of events as I hoped. I was already determined that my daughter should not lose her husband.

6

After King Henry had at last made his formal petition in 1231 to marry my sister Marjory, my husband's enemies tried to disgrace Hubert over the matter. They were already like slavering dogs about to overtake a stag, but had not yet brought it down. As for Henry, he wanted a wife and at the same time wanted Marjory, which in his instance was still like the desire of a worshipper for a statue of an angel, even of the Mother of God. Whether this worship could have ripened into everyday marriage I know not, and Marjory, serene in her beauty as always, merely smiled quietly, and said little.

It was decided against, I repeat, as there was already a double alliance with Scotland through the still childless Joan, Alexander's queen, and myself with Hubert. This was the danger, for if anything went amiss with my brother the king of Scots I was by right its queen, and Hubert would rule. It was at this point that his detractors spread sayings that could have been known, at first hearing, to be absurd; namely that Hubert himself had told Marjory the English king her suitor was 'a squint-eyed fool, a lewd man, a leper, deceitful, perjured, more faint-hearted than a woman, and utterly unfit for the company of any fair or noble lady.' Some of this was true about Henry III, but not all.

More adverse and unlikely tales began thereafter to circulate about my husband. It was as though his long and brave defence of Dover and the sally out to sea at Sandwich, the first of its kind in the late war, were forgotten. Hubert had poisoned, they said, the earl of Salisbury, Fair Rosamund's son who had saved Gascony; also an archbishop and one of the Marshal's sons; and had, of course, seduced myself with a view to the Scottish crown; that one raised its head time and again since our marriage. Hubert was a wizard, and had used charms to win the confidence of the young king; otherwise Henry was said to be terrified of him, having been burst in upon at Woodstock by the justiciar, breathing fierce threats and brandishing a drawn sword. Hubert had, they added, sent Llewelyn of Wales a precious stone which made him invulnerable in battle against England. My husband smiled at all this and continued with his daily business, but I began to be anxious.

Worse was to come. Hubert, they claimed, had appropriated the royal revenues; had given wardships to his kin and favourites; had sent overseas barrels filled with stones and sand instead of money he had kept, and which had been intended to aid the beleaguered magnates and burgesses of Poitou. The defections there were, as a result, Hubert's fault. (In fact the people of the region clearly preferred to adhere to France). As for King Henry's remaining possessions elsewhere in that debated land, the earl of Kent had been too greatly occupied with the fall of Fawkes de Bréauté to trouble to defend them. He had no right to the appointment of justiciar in the first place; it happened at a time of turmoil after Runnymede and had almost gone unnoticed. When was England not in turmoil? When did anyone tell the truth when it suited them not to? With Henry III like a reed swayed in the wind, hunting for a wife throughout Europe after Marjory was denied him, we were at the mercy of events and of Peter des Roches, whose insinuating ways flattered the king of England till he believed everything that was told him.

I cannot to this day understand how affection and trust, such as the young King Henry felt for my husband for many years, could turn without warning to black hatred and revenge almost as hellish as the hanging and then cutting down alive of besiegers who had been forced to surrender. There is no doubt that, occupied with great matters as Hubert was, he was left with less time to bear the king company for his diversion, which left room for others instead; but surely a foundation of liking remained, an awareness of all my husband had achieved since Dover? It is however possible, and has occurred to me as I lie awake at nights, that that very remembrance of a lengthy siege could be turned to suspicion of a possible secret understanding with France, giving young Louis time to gain allies and territory in south-east England.

My marriage is no doubt to blame for that, because of the memory of my father.

The Lion had made his private pact with old Louis VII as far back as 1170, with a view to a tripartite war against Henry II and a division of Henry's realm, returning Louis Normandy and the Angevin empire largely lost to France by the second nuptials of Eleanor of Aquitaine. Scotland also had had to suffer much from Henry II, in especial with regard to the northern counties and supposed vassalage by way of the late besotted Malcolm IV. A kinsman of my father's through Countess Ada's mother, who had been married first to the old earl of Leicester, brought in in those days a third ally, the then earl, known as Blanchemains; but that Leicester had a warlike wife. The Countess Peronelle arranged that Flemish troops should come by way of Wissant. That made a thrust from the eastward, my father and his brother David would attack from the north, and Henry II's son, who was at war with his father, would invade the south of England with ships and aid from France.

It was a grand design, but came to nothing for three causes. The winds from France were adverse, the intentions of the king's son wavered, and Hugh Bigod, at last deciding which side he was on, attacked the Flemish mercenaries with the aid of the East Anglian peasantry and left them heaped dead and rotting in ditches, to manure the next year's harvest. As for my father, the Lion was captured at Alnwick by the raising of a Northumbrian mist, said to be removed at the direct intervention of St Thomas Becket, to whom Henry II had prayed all night in penance before his shrine and been copiously flogged barefoot for a murder he had not, to do him justice, committed.

Prior to the Treaty of Canterbury with Coeur-de-Lion, which made void the Treaty of Falaise, father had been forced to sign for his very freedom in 1174. Scotland was England's admitted vassal for fifteen years, though the pope freed her church. My father's marriage, approved of by his overlord King Henry, did not take place till the year before that monarch's death and as I have made clear, was unwelcome to the Lion. However it got him his heir, who was now married to a barren queen from England. Certainly, the low-born de Burgh might hope to rule Scotland one day as king, especially with the aid of France. It was something to whisper into Henry III's ear; especially as he as yet had no wife or heirs of his own. Matters were set in train regarding this as soon as possible, my sister Marjory having been set aside: but she soon met Gilbert Marshal, and they fell in love.

This may be all surmise, out of my embittered mind; but I do not think so. The treatment to which my husband was subjected thereafter would have broken any man in the end.

7

My husband's fall was not swift, like Satan's. It was gradual, deliberately arranged, and was founded on Henry III's need to be diverted at all costs. I am not saying the king was all bad; nobody is so. He had the instinct to create, to beautify, to build; his new abbey is rising now, nearby where I sit. Nevertheless when left without some such matter to occupy his mind, it was open to evil counsel.

Everyday business wearied him, and Hubert had handled this well in the dozen or so years since the great Marshal had died. The reign, begun in such turmoil, had continued smoothly as water in a pond, and as a result Henry chafed for action, for war, for events and glorious achievements. The return of Peter des Roches from abroad unsettled him, with the bishop of Winchester's worldly talk of popes and emperors and the magnificence of Rome and Aix. The persuasive Poitevin voice would edge in concerning his known dislike for my husband, who in turn described Peter gruffly as vainglorious.

The whispering became open at last over the matter of forest lands. The Norman kings had made harsh laws for these, so that no man dared take royal game unbidden. Henry III now demanded that even land cleared and inhabited should be regarded as that of forest, and claimed fines from those who lived on it, causing them first to show by what warrant they held their houses. Someone, perhaps Peter and perhaps not, saw to it that Hubert was blamed for this unfair taxation, so that the common people began to see him as an oppressor. This was unjust; at the same time he was being blamed for having risen from among them.

About then, Henry wanted fame abroad, also to win back the lands his father had lost. His brother Richard had helped save Gascony with his kinsman Longsword of Salisbury at the age of sixteen, and the king was jealous. Henry had no such victory to his credit, and the thought made him chafe. Again my husband shouldered the blame, as after the brothers quarrelled Richard, by now earl of Cornwall, called an assembly of his peers and spoke up for himself according to English law. It was said Hubert had advised the king to exile his brother, though Hubert had no hand in any such advice. Despite Henry's threats of deporting him, Richard of Cornwall stayed in England, and was married by then to our Richard's widowed mother.

Henry, his mind set on war with France, prepared. My husband was against it, knowing too well the expense and bloodshed. He was however given the unwelcome task of fitting out the invading force. When the king's departure was delayed for other reasons, Henry flew into a rage and called Hubert a traitor to his face.

Ranulf of Chester, fancying himself as peacemaker, separated the two angry men. Hubert came home to me deeply disturbed and, for the first time, lacking in his usual quiet confidence. It was as though we walked on quicksand.

Yet another reason for trouble was my husband's distrust of papal legates, of whom he had no doubt seen enough in the previous reign. Hubert saw no reason for Italian power in England. The king, at this point, wrote to the new pope, Gregory IX, for support. Hubert protested, saying with truth that the English bishops had always supported Henry and were in any case near at hand to witness matters for themselves. His chaplain, Richard of St John, was in full agreement, but all of us missed the decisive voice of Stephen Langton, who was dead. It was as though God had withdrawn him in order to leave us in darkness.

Langton would however have supported the pope rather than permit lay power to rule the clergy. It was the old feud of the Norman kings against their primates: Stigand, Anselm, Becket, Langton himself. A short-lived bishop who only survived his consecration two years – Hubert was of course accused of poisoning him – denounced Hubert to the pope. My husband was no doubt in danger for making use of a force to which he had no rights. That was the kernel of it, and he knew it well enough, but was stubborn still.

At Christmas in Winchester, the season of goodwill, Hubert's fate was sealed. Peter des Roches was talking smoothly of how he had almost been named bishop of Damietta, in the service of the kings of Jerusalem, but for certain bungling. He blamed the pope and the emperor, but at the same time looked sideways at my husband. Mention of the East, of exotic things, fired the king; any word of Stupor Mundi, the excommunicated emperor, whom in other ways he strove to imitate, intoxicated Henry. Peter of Winchester broke in smugly to point out that he himself could never be excommunicated, as the great Innocent III had consecrated him personally in St Peter's.

The wine flowed at the feasting, and the pending disgrace of Ralph de Breton, who was my husband's treasurer and had been his chaplain, was talked of loudly at the high table. Also, for the first time, the name of Count Raymond of Provence, who had fair daughters and had made sweeping alterations in his own rule, was mentioned, with sullen looks still from the king. 'All I have are these Welsh wars,' he complained. 'No doubt profit is being made at your expense, sire, in such ways,' replied Peter, glib as oil. He must then have instructed Henry over the ensuing days regarding a new policy which would cause my husband to ruin himself.

It so happened about then that a man calling himself William Wither, but whose real name was Robert Tweng, collected a band of eighty young bravoes in the east parts of England who said they preferred to die rather than be confounded by the Romans. The document setting out their intentions was sealed with a device of two swords and the motto *Ecce duo gladii hic.* Monks of monasteries which had absent Italian superiors were warned to refuse to send their rents. Armed and masked, Wither's band moved swiftly about the countryside, emptying the barns of the Italians and giving the grain they stored to the poor, or else selling it. If challenged they showed royal letters patent, which were of course forged. Such Italians as they could lay hands on they seized, and kept prisoner.

All of this was approved greatly by the common people, who were tired of exactions. Naturally my husband was blamed at court for forging the letters patent.

They ferreted out what reasons they could. Hubert happened to have the knight's fee of one Peter de Brus in Foxholes, and Tweng came from there. My half-sister Isabel in Scotland had also married a de Brus. It was a slender connection and that first husband was long dead, but the name would be used to convince the king, with his ingrained suspicion of all Scots connections.

Pope Gregory was informed, and wrote a reproachful letter to king and prelates. He denounced, as might have been expected, the insults shown to papal envoys. He ordered the offenders to be excommunicated and sent to him for absolution, hardly a practical idea. It is possible that he did not know exactly where England was situated. He discoursed on the beauty of one fold and one shepherd, then ordered a general visitation throughout Canterbury. Needless to say, by the time his letters reached their destination it was far too late.

Henry III had acted. In a proclamation made before Yule he

informed the people of England that the insults to foreigners were due to the earl of Kent's misgovernment and the main cause of his dismissal as justiciar.

This followed. I will never forget Hubert's grey face. Peter des Roches had a son, known as Peter des Rivaux. He was made treasurer for life of the king's household. As a sop, my husband was given the justiciarship of Ireland. He never reached it. What happened next took place during a royal progress.

There was a holy cross at Bromholm, brought by a monk from Constantinople and said to be a relic of the True Cross, whose tree grew from one of the four seeds of Adam. Bromholm itself is a cell of the Cluniac priory at Castle Acre founded by the de Warennes, my kin. My husband had meantime exerted himself uselessly to try to bind the king, myself, the chancellor, treasurer and two stewards in a compact which was to do away with betrayal of any of us by any other. Henry signed it at Burgh itself, where Hubert had been born, I was present. There were smiles and civility, and, again, wine. I remember staring down at my rings.

A week later, at Shrewsbury, Hubert was ordered to surrender his castles. I understand that Henry wrote out an order to him to leave the country, but for some reason this was not sent. The justiciary of England was given to one Segrave, to whom my husband had lately made over several sheriffdoms. This man and his steward, Geoffrey of Crowcombe, then launched proceedings against the earl of Kent, Hubert de Burgh, my husband.

*

The law takes time. By the autumn there had been a foregathering of noble lords over the matter; old dying Ranulf, young Richard, Pembroke and Cognatus and Derby and the constable of Chester, whose name was de Lacy. Hubert was to be allowed to retire to the priory of Merton in Surrey to prepare his defence. However he would not meantime leave the place where he was, this being the place where I was also.

A mass of Londoners came down to attack like angry bees. Hubert fled and so did I. I rode straight, with Meggotta and a servant, and young Richard, to the abbey of St Edmund's Bury, where they knew us. Hubert tried to join us there, but was prevented. I can tell it starkly now.

He took refuge in the bishop of Norwich's house, which had its chapel. Hearing them come after him he made haste there by night in hope of sanctuary. They broke that, and entered the church itself to take him. They found him with the crucifix in one hand and the Host in the other, barefoot, having taken no time to put on his shoes and hose. They dragged him out and fettered him, and took him to the Tower.

It is said King Henry went to bed in peace when he heard the news.

8

What followed is shocking beyond belief.

The bishop of London, who was neither on one side nor the other, protested that sanctuary had been violated. Through his influence Hubert was allowed to return to it; not at Norwich, where I could in some way have reached him, but at a place where, in former days, a wood had been burned down. Burnt Wood, Brentwood, lies at a crossroads in Essex. There is a market held there on certain days. There were other diversions then for the time. Hubert's persecutors surrounded the place where he lay in sanctuary, and would allow no food to enter. Starved out, at last Hubert, by then almost a skeleton, surrendered to them and came forth into the light of day. There was a howl of triumph from the crowds; it only remained for them to cry 'Crucify him'. In ways, it had already been done.

They took him back to the Tower. He might as well never have left it. As was his habit he submitted quietly to the intolerable, agreed to whatever the king might desire, and arranged for such treasure as was held by him in the Temple to be transferred to the authorities of the crown, namely Peter the younger. He was tried on 10th November for crimes that still remained uncertain, which fact saved him.

The earl of Cornwall, Cognatus, Pembroke and de Lacy were again his judges. Within a few weeks de Lacy was made earl of Lincoln on the death, at last, of old Ranulf who had held that title with others. Meantime, at the trial, the king's mouth was set, his drooping eyelid twitching beneath his crown. Outside, the crowds swayed and murmured on. The earl of Kent had never courted popularity; he had not taken the leisure, but the king was not popular either.

One man dared to speak out in my husband's favour; the archbishop of Dublin, once Hubert's own confessor. He pointed out rightly that whatever it was my lord of Kent was supposed to have done in defiance of king and law, nobody seemed able to bring evidence of it. For that reason, I suppose, it was deemed impolitic to kill my husband.

The four earls agreed in the end to imprison him at Devizes, the strong castle where in days of old, both Robert Curthose and, later, the terrible Robert de Bellême had been held. Hubert lost his lordships and offices, but retained his private lands and his dignity as earl and baron. Perhaps, after all, the fact that I was his wife stood him in some stead. To denude him utterly, or make threats against his life, might have aroused action from Scotland, where I was after all not forgotten.

Hubert languished in Devizes for more than a year.

Meggotta, little Richard de Clare and I remained together in sanctuary at St Edmund's Bury.

One thing comforted me in all this, besides the children. Hubert was a Norfolk man, and the Norfolk smith to whom they took him after breaking the first sanctuary refused to put on his fetters. They had to find another, who did not know him. In other words, those who themselves knew the great justiciar, his honesty and industry, whether or not they were friends to William Wither and his masked men, would not act against him despite risking the wrath of the king. In time, I knew, Hubert's worth would be acknowledged and the lack of it in others seen for what it was. Nevertheless, all of that year he lay chained in a dungeon, and I was not permitted either to see him or hear from him.

I wrote among others to my brother Alexander, the king of Scotland. *For God's love, save the earl of Kent.* I told him of all that had befallen, and that my daughter and I were in sanctuary. I did not mention young Richard, lest the letter be found and his presence remembered, and removed.

Gradually, the four knights who guarded my husband at Devizes must have come to know that the quiet man they kept in chains, by the king's order allowed to see nobody but his confessor, could by no reckoning be the monster of avarice and deceit that had been implied. Watching someone day after day allows truth to reveal itself in small things. Hubert's way was never to resist, never to chafe, and expostulate, and give way to petulant rages, like the king. His faith reminded him of what St Paul had said, that neither height nor depth, princes nor prison could keep Christ out. He had committed no crime and accordingly made no defence. That was his stance, then and later; like the man of Tarsus himself.

During the year one of the knights petitioned to be allowed to go elsewhere, and in this way I was able to obtain news of my lord's health. He was fettered, but the calm of his mind prevented his beating his fists against the walls, or his head, as many did, driving themselves mad or else to death. Hubert had taken counsel of the Dominicans for some time, and practised their discipline of thought. One way and another, and with my own careful relating of the real state of things where I might, by the year's end those who had been against Hubert were mostly for him, not only in Devizes but in all England.

Meantime King Henry held a great council at Merton, where it was fashionable to make endowments since the time of King John. John's son kept in his hands certain matters which by the Great Charter should have been distributed fairly. One was watch and ward against convicted offenders. Another was mantle-children born before wedlock, but present at their parents' wedding and covered by the nuptial cloth. There was argument about whether they were, or were not, thereafter legitimate. In either case, they themselves can have been left with few uncertainties. Such matters had never troubled my father the old Lion, and did not trouble me. Meggotta and Richard were brought up from the beginning to know about such things and how they happened.

Weighty discussions were held concerning all of that at

Merton, and I forget what the conclusions were, being naturally more concerned with the effect on my husband's fate of what turned out to be the first crack in the smooth defences of Peter des Roches. I watched the bishop of Winchester's fall at last with unchristian gratification. His probable son, Peter des Rivaux, evaded the royal wrath; he was a dogged worker who showed everything in writing and did not flaunt himself, or try to climb high. As a result he was kept on in his lifetime's appointment as the king's treasurer, and was not among the crowd of Poitevins who began to cause trouble that year and after.

They were, as stated, the second family of Queen Isabelle, with their retainers. Many of these married noble Englishwomen as I say and acquired their titles, and one bride was even taken out of a nunnery to copy her sister, who had been united with one of these dedicated climbers. Likewise, the daughters of the queen herself found noble English husbands. It was a quieter conquest than that of Hastings, but as lasting. The king himself was still casting about for a wife, and when he found one it made everything worse.

The baronage as a whole feared foreign influence, which is odd when one remembers that they themselves, if they had any position in the land, had come originally from abroad. One or two of the descendants of old Ethelred II, the Confessor's royal sire, survived quietly and bred, mostly in Scotland; but on the whole the aristocracy was Norman.

The master of the Temple had meantime, among all this,

handed over Hubert's treasure to the king. I felt nothing; it did not matter to me that our great cup with figures in carved relief, and my gold brooch set with sapphires and garnets, were gone, and my coronet as countess of Kent. I was more concerned with Kent's earl, held deep in prison for no crime. I recalled how they had tried to force him to take Templar vows, which would have discredited our marriage; they had attempted that already by saying Hadwisa and I were in close consanguinity through old Henry Beauclerc. 'I told them I knew nothing of that,' Hubert said to me afterwards; yes, I was to see him again.

The king spent our money from the Temple, but needed more for his own warlike plans, also to pay for the marriage of his sister Isabella to the emperor, Stupor Mundi. He levied a heavy tallage on the Jews, and made laws concerning their rate of interest on loans. There are few other means than moneylending open to these unfortunate people. Henry had piously built a home for converted ones between Holborn and the river, but I cannot think it had many inmates. They are as tenacious of their faith as we, and I heard one tale only lately. A Jew fell into a privy on a Saturday, which is their sabbath, and an earl offered to pull him out, but was not suffered to, as Jewish law forbade. On Sunday the Jew asked to be pulled out, but by then it was the earl's sabbath and he refused. By Monday, the Jew was dead. The earl concerned was my Richard, grown to be a man. There are those who can laugh at the tale, but after what happened later I cannot.

That apart, Jews who could not be of service to the king

were requested to leave the realm. It is hard to know where they may safely lay their heads; in Spain, I believe they were formerly castrated if found to be circumcised, even as young children.

Meantime, the last son of the great Marshal to remain alive came home.

The Marshal had had five sons, and as many daughters, by his wife, who was herself the heiress of Strongbow, and Strongbow had married in his time the daughter of the king of Leinster. I like to remember that long and magical line of ancestry; Ireland was forgotten in living memories here before a pope granted it to Henry II as a see of the English church, which was the last thing needed; the Irish missionaries had spread all over Europe from long before, having been taught by Greeks who earlier visited their country and brought much learning, and such as Columba continued the tradition carried away from our own islands at the coming of the Saxons, who drove out the Celts and Christianity as it had first come by way of early Rome. No doubt, in the end, the two sides rejoined one another, but by then there were differences. I never discussed this matter much with my husband, who was a plain devout Englishman of the usual kind. My own blood contains rebellious Celtic traces from old Ceann Mór, and those before him.

The Marshal's son Richard had lived in France, and soon became spokesman for the baronage. He had an honest tongue, like his father. Our chaplain at St Albans, Father Lawrence, who kept in touch with us, said Richard Marshal thought and acted like my husband and shared Hubert's views by very nature. This fact was cheering.

Meantime death had been busy; not, thank God, at Devizes or St Edmund's, but along the Marches and in Wales. The old hanging of de Braose, Llewelyn's wife's lover, had put paid to that lady's mediations with her half-brother King Henry, as her lord kept her in prison for a long time.

Llewelyn's war, therefore, for lack of information, had been blamed on my husband, with its expenses. The new Earl Marshal however detested Peter des Roches, and Llewelyn was ready to aid him.

It was about then that an unexpected and pleasant thing happened; an old mistress of my father the Lion came to me, the one who had long ago borne him his son Robert of London. She was agile for her years, had heard of our trouble and asked if she might serve me. She – her name was Maud – had money, for my father had been generous while he lived, and her son in the north still kept her with enough on which to stave off poverty: but she would not go to him in Scotland, as she said she had heard it was a cold place and she liked to be warm.

'I can handle a flat-iron, lady, and wash your linen and the little lady's and my young lord's. I used to be a laundress when I took up with your royal father, and he with me. It was in the days when he used to ride down now and again to spend Easter with old King Henry, before the quarrel. A fine strong man in bed, your father the king was. I started Robert after the first night with him. He used to ride often to see me after that, from Woodstock.' She remembered how angry the Lion had been when in the end, after imprisonment and forced vassalage, he had had to take a bride of King Henry II's choosing. 'I saw her for myself, the good lady, escorted north by her brother as she was, for the Lion wouldn't go with her, but came to me instead, straight after his grand wedding at Woodstock and free hunting in the king's forest for the week. He didn't take to her even after you was born, or the next or the next, as I know for I saw him three times after. After *that*, they tell me, with the fine prince she gave him at last, he knew his queen's value, but I'm telling you what you know already. What you maybe don't know is that when he rode off next day from me at the time, he took young Robert north on his saddle-bow, to show everyone he cared nothing. He was a stubborn great Norman, and so I told him. I was never afraid of him, but always respectful, knowing he was a king.'

She would rattle on so, and I liked to hear her talk of my parents, for my mother Queen Ermengarde had died two years after seeing all of us married at York. It passed the sad waiting days to hear about things I partly remembered, but had perhaps not fully understood.

Also, it was of use to have a serving-woman who would stay with us in sanctuary. By the time we left it, old Maud was a part of the family as a retainer, with her memories and her useful ways with the flat-iron. She died not long since, at a great age, still with her wits, and in Scotland after all, with her son.

By Pentecost the king of England was at Gloucester and Feckenham, eating fresh fish from the ponds there. He ordered, in his sullen peevish way, a proclamation in every shire court, in hundreds, at fairs and markets, that watch was to be kept every night, in every vill, by four or more men, till Michaelmas. Anyone who could not give a good account of himself was to be pursued with hue and cry. Lodging for more than one night was to be denied to any stranger who could not find pledges, and such men, if arrested, were to be held for trial by itinerant justices, though it might well be some time before the latter came that way. Magna Carta might never have been signed. Within two weeks the Marcher barons were forced to give hostages for their loyal service as in the days of the king's father, 'until the realm is so safe that there is firm peace in England.' Henry had had firm peace once, and had imprisoned its guardian.

The Earl Marshal himself, along with Cognatus and others, was one of the guarantors of Hubert's safe confinement, in other words of the knights who guarded him. As they 'had not been obedient to the king' – in other words were beginning to have sympathy with their prisoner – they themselves were to be placed under surveillance by the king's knights and crossbowmen. Henry III was weaving a most tangled web for himself. A man of the locality named Gilbert Bassett, who owned the manor of Compton, was named to the king as dangerous, and his house, if necessary, was to be destroyed with the aid of the sheriff and his men. Otherwise, everyone's horses and gear were to be taken away. Henry can no longer have spent peaceful nights in his bed; he must have thought it all out in the small hours.

Gilbert Bassett was in fact our mainstay. I had been in touch with him. He was a friend of the Marshal and an enemy of Peter des Roches, as was his henchman Richard Siward. Whether or not this Siward was of the ancient blood of Northumbria I know not, only that he was staunch. In the late summer of 1233, the year after Hubert's arrest, both these lords – Siward was married to the dowager countess of Warwick – repudiated their allegiance to the king. Disinherited and outlawed, they roamed the countryside with their war bands, in some manner like William Wither and his men in the east parts, but this was in the west.

They proclaimed openly to all that they suffered for the cause of Hubert de Burgh, earl of Kent. In the previous year such a state of things would not have been possible.

At first they had the ear of Richard of Cornwall, the king's brother, but though he and Henry as usual did not agree he reverted to allegiance; Richard was prudent, and already had an eye to a future beyond seas. There was a colloquy held at Wycombe, one of Bassett's own manors. Roger Bigod of Norfolk, who two years later shamefully married my sister Isabel, at this point made his peace in the weathervane fashion of his family.

The king then decided to ban all tournaments; certainly these can inflame the passions unduly. In addition, the late proclaiming of watch and ward meant a collection of levies on the roads to the Marches. Flemish troops, which had meantime arrived from the south, strengthened the king's hand in as much as mercenaries may. At the same time there followed friendly discussions with Llewelyn, who had taken his wife out of prison.

Henry then decided that he was free to go to Ireland. Ships for this purpose were to collect at Ilfracombe and Milford Haven. The knight-service of England was to gather at Gloucester.

Suddenly the king changed his mind, and announced that he would attack the Marshal brothers, of whom four were then still alive.

At that time in Ireland Hubert's nephew, Richard de Burgh, was himself at odds with the old Marshal's remaining sons. Whether the name of de Burgh itself reminded the king that my husband still lived, or not, it was one step nearer to Hubert's return to trust, if that is the term with such a king.

Henry however continued to behave like a man who cannot make up his mind. Having given orders that Richard Marshal, the eldest surviving brother, was to be resisted if he carried war into Ireland, the king stayed at home after all. He moved to Hereford, ordering the Severn passages to be strictly watched, and then laid siege to the Marshal's castle at Usk. Marshal – it was both his surname and his title – agreed formally to surrender it and to receive it again with fifteen days, a not unusual arrangement. At that rate the king was to amend, with the bishops' counsel, whatever needed correcting in his kingdom, by then a good deal.

However though the Marshal journeyed as far as Woodstock on his way to a council at Westminster with the king, word reached him that his Usk castle had not yet been restored. He rightly feared treachery, and the truce was ended. The king thereafter continued to destroy the Marshal's castles and manors in England as far as he might, but by this time Richard Marshal had recovered Usk, and with our friends Bassett and Siward, also by now Llewelyn in person, carried the war into South Wales.

Fierce fighting raged in this fashion until January, despite the winter. The Marshal and Llewelyn captured and burnt Shrewsbury. The king had his hired Flemings, but they could do little despite their able commander the Comte des Guisnes, as knight-service in England could not be relied on. The king's forces were defeated so often that he appealed to the men-at-arms of the border shires to come to his aid in return for wages, as though they had been mercenary troops. Henry himself remained inactive at Gloucester, in company with Peter des Roches, no longer the mouthpiece of God. The king had not in fact enough forces, raised by whatever means, to face the increasing resentment against his rule. The common people's state during all this was piteous; I heard of it in sanctuary, and did what I might.

Henry began to bluster presently and said he would not make peace with the Marshal unless the latter came as a confessed traitor with a rope round his neck. Calmer counsel prevailed elsewhere. A few days before Christmas, in Glamorgan in the Cistercian abbey there, the Marshal had received Brother Agnellus of the new order of Minorites, the Franciscans. This much respected friar had known the saint of Assisi himself; our preoccupations with property and lands must have seemed alien. In his grey-brown habit the friar nevertheless made his way through the wintry land, catching a chill in the process which shortly killed him. However he was given time to assure the Marshal of safely and provision in Herefordshire if he would submit.

The entire field of dissent having thus been gone over in detail, it was proved beyond doubt that the government of the bishop of Winchester was most evil. In the end the king succumbed, and des Roches was confounded utterly, but kept his life.

I knew little of all this directly. It is probable that my brother Alexander of Scots was already involved, and certainly so by the next move; after all war is a game of blood-stained chess. The Dominican Robert Bacon, a great scholar of Oxford, had told Henry III roundly that peace was impossible as long as the bishop of Winchester remained in power. Others vociferously agreed, including the bishop of London who had already denounced the violation of sanctuary when my lord was dragged away. Also, it so happened that another bishop had been manhandled on attempting to leave England; and there had been the starvation of Hubert out of second sanctuary. If these unprincipled ways were to repeat themselves, there was no justice.

Bacon produced a strongly worded letter from the pope in support of Hubert and myself. This was most heartening, and almost certainly due to my brother King Alexander II. Peter des Roches in his days of power had sneered, when bishops and friars remonstrated with the king, that there were no peers of his left in England. By now, there was a better man chosen than he; the pope's own candidate, Edmund of Abingdon.

There had been great difficulty in finding a new archbishop of Canterbury on the death of Stephen Langton. The king had favoured two well-known men and their prior, but all three failed to satisfy Pope Gregory. It is believed that Simon Langton, the dead Stephen's brother and archdeacon, sent local knowledge to Rome: one candidate was not learned enough, another too old, the third too greatly under the influence of Peter des Roches. In the end, as had happened last time, the pope discarded all three and selected his own man, Edmund.

Edmund of Abingdon is so well known and respected that I need say little; except that, after Paris and Oxford, he forswore the teaching of theology, in which he had excelled, because he said that to keep winning arguments made him too pleased with himself. Like others before him he accepted the see with reluctance, but this always had to appear to happen.

Meantime, after a painful scene at Westminster between rival supporters of Marshal and king, a foregathering of bishops contrived to induce in Henry III a sense of the error of his ways. His reply was to go, again, on pilgrimage to the True Cross relic at Bromholm. Perhaps he remembered the earlier one, and the company,

Three men went with him this time, two of whom were about to be got rid of. They were Peter des Roches, still clinging grimly on, his son Peter, who as already said survived in office, and Stephen Segrave. Henry, having shrived his soul, continued his journey by way of Walsingham, then Castle Acre among the Cluniacs, a foundation of Cognatus' ancestors. After stopping at Ramsey and Peterborough he then began negotiations for peace with the Marshal and Llewelyn.

Archbishop-elect Edmund and his suffragans sent the bishops of Coventry and Rochester with terms, which Henry accepted in March. Edmund's consecration took place in April, and thereafter he undertook to join the two named bishops in treating with Llewelyn.

At this point news came that the Marshal himself was dead in Ireland, of his wounds, as I have already stated.

There is little doubt that he was done to death by treachery. He had sailed to quell trouble in his lands of Leinster as soon as affairs seemed to be settling in England. Richard de Burgh and Maurice Fitzgerald were waging war and had seized some of his castles. The Marshal contrived to recapture several before an arrangement, made by way of the Templars, was made for all leaders to meet together at the Curragh to discuss a truce. A larger force than his own met the Marshal there, fighting broke out and he was wounded, but recovered enough to play dice in his tent. A surgeon, called to inspect the wounds, plunged a red-hot iron into them, and as I have said Richard Marshal died raving in the resultant fever. King Henry, when he heard the news, said he mourned wholeheartedly. In fact he probably knew well enough that Llewelyn and Siward would be disturbed by the death.

As for Peter des Roches, he was told to have his financial receipts in order and thereafter to take himself to France. This was officially to treat for peace, but he was better out of the country after what had resulted from his presence in it. He was in fact saved from destruction by the intervention of his fellow bishops, not to be the last in such a state.

I must go back now in memory, a long way; to the time, two years before, that the three of us, myself and my daughter and young Richard de Clare, had fled to sanctuary in St Edmund's Bury, having been separated from my husband.

We travelled in my litter, without cognizance. There was a moment's fear on the journey, as we came at last in sight of the famous abbey and its rearing strawberry-coloured tower. Among the jumble of traffic before the abbot's bridge a second litter swayed towards us, grandly decked and bearing the de Warenne wyvern on its banners. I did not know which side Cognatus was on, or if it was indeed he or the Marshaless. I kept the curtains closed, and we made way humbly for the other equipage, as if to greater folk than we. Whoever it was – I think Cognatus himself would more likely have been in the saddle, with trumpets blaring at his approach – with dusk falling, we approached the gateway, and its small door to one side for sanctuary-seekers, which I had never foreseen I would have cause to enter. I climbed out and took Meggotta in one hand and Richard in the other, hastening them in. I had bidden the guards leave our small gear and take the litter back home. I did not know when I would see it again, or the men. I knocked, with the urgent knocking of the suppliant. It was possible, I knew, that there might be thieves and murderers sheltering here; all such could claim sanctuary from the law and the king's power. I was ready, with thick clothing to defend myself and the children. Any sharp knives would be taken from us as not to be used in the house of God.

It seemed a long time before the grille opened, and a lay-brother's shaven face surveyed us, eyes squinting above his held lantern. It threw the shadows upwards, making his face a demon's. I remembered that what he would see in turn would be a haggard woman in a frieze cloak, and two bewildered children.

'Who comes?' he said, for he did not know me. They do not ask what offence one has committed. I replied that I was the countess of Kent, that they had taken my lord for no cause, and that I and my young daughter and the earl's ward were all three in need of sanctuary.

The door creaked open then, and we saw a stone passage, without light except for the lantern, which gave off acrid smoke. It was like entering prison.

However a monk came soon, and remembered me and my lord, and that we had been benefactors. He made us welcome, and by mercy gave us a private cell with empty pallets. The children were tired with the journey and I put them to bed. I myself sought out the chapel, to pray for Hubert's safety wherever he now was. At that moment, the smith was refusing to weld his fetters.

Before the high altar there was a kneeling figure, a false moneyer who shared our refuge. He did us no harm. At that time there was much clipping of money, and Richard of Cornwall later made vast sums out of the king his brother by allowing him tin from the Cornish mines to make alloy. However my mind at that time was far from considering such things. The abbot received me and, again, said that we were welcome.

When I returned from my prayers and visiting the abbot, the two children were lying asleep in one another's arms. I think it was then that I devised my plan, though I did not yet know for certain that when they could secure him, they would take Richard away. Meantime, he was safe with us; and if the pair were married at once, young as they were, they could continue to sleep together until, in nature and affection, it had become a full marriage.

I had not brought much money with me, as my steward would be able to arrange such matters with the abbey's mint. As soon as might be, I also arranged for letters to be written and messengers sent, in the first place, to my brother the king of Scots. I knew Alexander would aid Hubert; the pair had liked one another at York in '21. Also, it being scarcely a year since King Henry had petitioned to be allowed to marry our sister Marjory, no doubt friendly feeling still prevailed.

Regarding that, the king of England's advisers having told him to look elsewhere, Henry entangled himself about then with Ponthieu, making a bid for the count's daughter Joanna. In fact he committed himself too deeply, then found it difficult to change direction, with the result that he became known through Europe as a bridegroom who could not keep his word. It became difficult for him to find a wife.

No word came from Alexander, and I realized with despair that he must be dealing with rebellions and pretenders in the further parts of his kingdom. Claimants to the throne still abounded in Scotland among those who resented the inheritance of Margaret Atheling, whom they called the Saxon woman even by then. Moreover Alexander's English wife had as yet borne him no heir. All other things being equal, I might have a future king and queen of Scots in my charge, sleeping in one another's arms. The prospect did not leave me.

9

I saw Meggotta and Richard de Clare married secretly, before the altar of St Edmund's Bury by my chaplain and our friend, Father Lawrence of St Albans, who came at my urgent request. It would not have been politic to ask any of the clerics of St Edmund's itself to officiate. Before he came, I talked with the two children solemnly; reminded them that broad lands on both sides were a part of the contract, and that a royal inheritance might, in time, be Richard's if heirs to Scotland failed. 'You must say nothing of that,' I told them, already knowing young Richard's eagerness to amass possessions. It was not an attractive trait, but would serve. I told Father Lawrence the truth, that this marriage was the wish of Richard's guardian; that was before the king had retrieved the position for himself, in the following year, too late.

I saw them kneel together, those two children, and exchange rings I had had fashioned at the mint. I did not reproach myself; the late King John had married and bedded a child; shortly his son was to take a bride of twelve years and do the same. This time the bridegroom was his wife's exact age, and we must therefore wait a little. I heard the nuptial mass said over them, and afterwards we had a little feast together in our cell; other luxuries were there by then, including a great tented bath made of slatted wood, into which my servants would pour hot water from the brazier. The pair would share this, splashing and laughing together. We were crowded, a little, but not uncomfortable; and we could receive visitors when they came.

One of the first was Cognatus, blowing out his cheeks with self-importance. He regretted the situation in which I found myself, regretted it very much. 'My wife will visit you,' he promised, and without doubt meant it. He asked about the progress of the boy Richard and I said he was doing well under the instruction of the clerks at Bury. The sixth earl remarked that he would require other instruction in time. 'He is not to be a monk, but a warrior and great lord. He should learn to tilt at the ring, and the finer points of horsemanship, and how to fly a merlin meantime. It cannot be done from here, in sanctuary.' He said the word as if it was distasteful, as if I had lowered my status; no doubt I had. I countered with a suggestion that in a little while, Richard should perhaps learn to tilt with staves, which could be done without danger in the abbey precinct. 'Other boys may come presently,' I said, 'to match him in skills.' The earl mentioned Hubert's stepson Bardolf, who had a place in his household, being of near kin.

'He is older,' I said. 'Send him in a little while.'

We drank wine, and Cognatus rode off, for once without pomp. No doubt he meant well.

Richard and Meggotta played happily together in each other's company as the months passed, roaming round the great abbey hand in hand, staring at the carved images and the gleam of gold and silver offerings on the altar where they had been married. I told them the story of St Edmund, whose relics were here and who had been martyred long ago by the Danes for refusing to renounce his Christian faith. Two hundred years afterwards the Danish king of England, Cnut, tried to atone for his countrymen's murder by building this fine abbey in the martyr's honour. The children listened to that and other stories I told them, Richard learned his Latin from the clerks and Meggotta her stitches from me, and the friendly lay-brother who had admitted us, no longer resembling a demon by now, showed them a game he said the Romans used to play, with coins shoved in squares ruled out on the ground or else the dust. 'They say they played it above the sweet Lord's head while he was confined in a cell below, the night he had been taken and was to appear before Pilate in the morning,' he told them. Such tales abounded since the return of warriors from the Holy Land, who had seen for themselves the places in Jerusalem. 'I should like,' said Meggotta one day, 'to see the little rock from which Our Lord ascended into heaven. The good brother says they have built a church round it, though it's quite small. What would you like to see, Richard?'

Richard said he would like to see the Holy Lance, which had been found by a miracle at Antioch. Such things passed our days pleasantly enough, if it had not been for my constant fear for my husband.

In as far as I could, I taught the young pair how to conduct themselves in the great world when, as must surely happen, they returned to court. I taught them courtly dances, such as my sisters and I had learned when we first came to England. I would watch while Richard, ever growing taller and stronger, picked Meggotta up by the waist in the dance's prescribed figures, and twirled her round above his head, the pair laughing happily. 'When we have music it will be better still,' I said.

The answer to my letter to Alexander came to me at last in the form of his queen, my fellow-bride from York on the unforgotten day. Joan rode south often, preferring her native land to the one she had failed and which evidently disliked her. 'The cold never leaves my bones there,' she said, her mouth drooping. She said my brother was well, but forever busied with Galloway and the Isles. It sounded as if they did not seek one another's company unduly. Nevertheless Joan brought a gift which we opened with joy; a chess-set, carved in Moray of narwhal ivory. Thereafter I taught the two children to play, and it profited them greatly. I can see, even now, Meggotta's intent little face bent over the board, and her fingers, one of which bore Richard's ring, shyly moving bishops and knights and queens.

Joan that day had brought with her her youngest sister Eleanor, who was perhaps the most beautiful of King John's daughters, with her mother's golden hair hidden beneath the tied veil of an anchoress. Eleanor had been the wife of the eldest Marshal, William, and at his death had elected to take vows never to remarry. I thought this was a pity; Eleanor was a desirable woman, and did not strike me as in the least nunlike, but the vows were already taken. She sat in silence, her long gold-tipped lashes resting on her cheeks. Her fate was in fact to be far different from that of her present intent. Some years later, after scandal which of course said he had seduced her, she was married a second time to a persuasive young French noble named Simon de Montfort. His charm had already caused old Ranulf to surrender to him, for no charge, the earldom of Leicester.

After the two had gone I remembered that Eleanor's late Marshal had been turbulent, and had earlier wanted, as the king did, to marry Marjory. Perhaps Henry's moods and Eleanor's sudden vows were to be accounted for by early unhappiness; it cannot have been a contented royal family, and Queen Isabelle had made haste to return to her original betrothed at John's death. Hubert, in fact, had been in Portugal to try to arrange a marriage earlier for King John, at the time that monarch reft Isabelle away without warning from Hugh de la Marche. Now, the harvest was being reaped in the form of too many Poitevins. All this was before the arrival of the Provençals and the Savoyards, those last also resulting from Henry III's eventual marriage in 1235.

10

In stated gratitude to Richard de Burgh, for services in Ireland, the king at last arranged for the consideration of my husband's freedom. The cold words warmed my heart.

At the same time Henry fined those in Ireland who had taken the Marshal's part. It was increasingly evident that Henry's right hand knew not what his left hand did. Letters under the royal seal, for which as a youth Henry himself had so ardently striven, were said to have been sent to Ireland to contrive Richard Marshal's death; and one Geoffrey de Marisco, outwardly his friend, was likewise said to have been in the plot. It ended, if such things ever end, with the disappearance of most of those involved and the flight of Geoffrey to sanctuary at Clerkenwell, while his son turned pirate and thereafter made raids from Lundy Island, nursing deep hatred against the king.

If Henry murdered the Marshal it was a crime indeed. He had to blame some other, and as Peter des Roches was available the king turned on him as he had once turned on my husband. The bishop of Winchester was again saved from destruction by the pleas of his fellow-bishops.

All of it mattered less to me than my husband's release from prison.

When I saw him again, I embraced a man much aged, stiff in the joints and with ankles scarred and swollen from the fetters he had worn ever since capture. When we were alone, he told me, lying in my arms, of the events of the past intolerable year.

'As you know, I did not plead,' Hubert said. 'Had I done so, and judgment been passed against me, I would have been outlawed and all would have been lost. To do nothing, say nothing, gave my friends time to plead for me to the king in person, and was best; Henry is not steadfast either in hate or love.'

'You should have spared yourself,' I said, stroking his hair; it had turned grey. 'We would have been welcomed in Scotland.'

'And caused war? I am no man's penniless and landless supplicant.'

I reached out for the wine-cup, which stood beside our bed, and made him take a long draught to bring the colour back into cheeks still pale from prison. 'I don't doubt,' Hubert continued, 'that Cognatus spoke up for us when it was safe. We were allowed by the end to keep the lands not held in chief of the crown.'

'Crowns mean little,' I said, my cheek against his, 'Rest now. Tomorrow we will rub your joints with a soothing oil.'

He smiled. 'Had I become a Templar as they demanded, there would have been no oil and little soothing. Can you see me as one? Had I agreed to that, they'd have let me go free, saying no farewell either to you or Meggotta. She has grown.' They had earlier met, and embraced. 'Good Bassett saved me, after the king had blockaded the castle at Devizes for fear his orders were being disobeyed,' Hubert went on. 'The bishop of Dublin, always a friend to us as you know, was allowed in to shrive my soul when I asked for it, also to bring me news. That was that Peter des Roches was trying to persuade the king to give him custody of Devizes, for my greater safe keeping. That itself meant that I would never again have seen the light of day.'

I shuddered, and clung to him. 'Thank God it did not happen so,' I said. 'My prayers from sanctuary saved you.'

He made little of the conditions at Devizes, the food sent grudgingly to the cell door, the everlasting fetters; the sudden withdrawal of Richard of Cornwall's chief knight, and the anxiety about who would replace him. 'After that, I persuaded those who had charge of me,' Hubert said quietly. In the first watch of the night of Michaelmas they had lifted him on their shoulders, still fettered as they could not remove the gyves. They carried him thus to the parish church, to sanctuary. 'We were followed,' Hubert said. 'I heard them being dragged back as soon as I was inside. They say the news reached Henry next day at Oxford. There must have been hard riding through the night.' His voice was dry.

'No doubt he was enraged, as by custom,' I said. 'He is like his father, but without John's resolution in adversity. Instead he gives in to that, and turns to his prayers.'

'Well, prayer did not avail him notably: he ordered sanctuary to be broken again. I was to be returned to my cell and fastened with three rings of iron, and allowed speech with no man.'

'He is a monster. Such a one should not rule.'

'Well, the bishop of Salisbury heard of the violation, and that the guards dared not again return me to the church. They said, and one can understand it, that they would sooner see me hanged than hang themselves. They had done what they might, and no man can do more.' He sounded almost amused; he had not described the second seizure in the church at Devizes.

'The bishops conferred on all of it,' I said. 'We heard as much at St Edmund's Bury.' Father Lawrence had kept me informed of such matters, either coming himself from St Albans or sending a trusted clerk.

'They conferred, excommunicated my friends the guards and took 'em to court. By then the world knew of it. I was duly taken back to the church again, still in my fetters. In a way, I miss them; their presence stimulated my mind.'

'My poor lord,' I said.

'Why, that is only half of it. Next, the sheriff was ordered to appear at Devizes with the coroner and the whole force of the shire. It is evident that a fettered man can be dangerous.'

'You were only so for thwarting the king's will.'

'Let it be. They were to be there be early morning on St Luke's day, and were to watch the church day and night. The king lets few folk sleep. I had a certain entertainment, looking out at a window, having helped myself up with my hands, like a cripple.'

He moved a little, as if it was still not to be credited that he could freely do so again. 'Never ask how Bassett and Siward got in to me,' he said. 'They contrived it despite all the stir, and rode off with me to safety, here, in the Marshal's country. We were all of us outlawed, naturally. Nevertheless the great meeting of the council reversed the outlawry, saying it was unjust and contrary to the law of the land.'

I nodded, remembering Magna Carta. Outlawry at the king's suit is null and void unless an inquest has been taken by the justices, and the fugitive found guilty as the result either of indictment or appeal. In Hubert's case there had been neither.

'So now you are restored to the king's grace and love.' I spoke with irony.

'Ay.' He frowned a little. 'I would have a word with you about that, but not now. Set your lips on mine again, unless the taint of prison is still on my breath. I had some fresh air in Wales, before I saw the king.'

'You saw Henry?'

'Let us cease to talk of Henry. I have lacked your love for more than a year, my wife.'

*

In the dawn hours he began to talk again. 'I do not want to grieve Meggotta,' he said. 'You must break this news to her; I cannot. The king, who himself fostered the notion at the beginning, made me swear on oath that she will not now marry Richard de Clare.'

The blood went back to my heart. I left our bed and put on my gown, and made pretence to rinse my face and hands. Hubert talked on, saying it was time he himself rose and saw to many affairs which had silted up in his absence. 'Henry led me up to the altar at Gloucester after the archbishop and the rest, who had made peace between us, had departed,' he said. 'He swore that I should never have his favour if I promoted the marriage, and made me swear on oath that I would not. It may be the ill-feeling with Richard's stepfather the king's own brother, or Henry may have designed Richard for a foreign bride, like so many. Margaret, why are you pale? The child will marry some other; we still have lands.'

I flung myself at his feet, his poor feet swollen still, and forever scarred from the shackles. 'My lord, they are married,' I told him. 'It was my doing; I feared to lose him for her; and matters have now gone too far to undo.'

He was silent for instants. Then 'You mean they have lain together? She is as pretty, our girl, as a newly opened rose.'

'Yes. It happened at Hertford on the way. It was my doing, as I say. He was ready, she was not; but I made her obey me.' She had bled, my little daughter; but I had talked to her earlier of the duties of marriage. Her parts were a child's still, and it had hurt her. Richard was manly for his age, and I had heard him boast earlier to Bardolf and the rest that he was ready, and they had laughed and said he was too young. Nevertheless there had been the act of marriage between them, and I and Maud had witnessed it from behind the curtain.

'Have I ruined you, and our child?' I asked now, and broke down and wept. I seldom weep, and had not done so all through the time of great trouble; but now my tears bathed his feet like Christ's. I felt his hands reach out and lift me up.

'Whatever happens now, we are together,' he said. 'I will not be separated from you again.'

We decided that the king had best know nothing till he had to. I had brought Meggotta with me to welcome her father, leaving the boy Richard de Clare at Hertford. Since then I have bitterly regretted that also; had I kept the young pair together it might not have been as easy to alter Richard's mind. He has since been compared to Paris in his youth, and the beauty and grace of his limbs; Ulysses in his shrewdness, Aeneas in his piety – he has lately been taken with a desire to go on many pilgrimages – and Hector in his strength and feats of arms. Young as he then was I have another name for Richard de Clare, earl of Gloucester, who is also known for his avarice. It is Judas.

That time, when I had dried my tears and had myself dressed, I went to Meggotta. Early as it still was in the day, she was seated industriously sewing fringe on a tunic for her young husband, as a name-day gift. She adored Richard and praised everything he did. I took her hand and bade her put down her needle.

'You must not see him again for the time,' I told her. 'Have patience and keep silent. Your father is not yet out of danger.'

Her face whitened, and it was as though I had struck her; but she asked no questions. I left her, no longer able to bear the sight of the harm I had done; and went to the chapel, to my prayers. Perhaps, I thought, I was no better than King Henry, who turned assiduously to his whether or not all else had failed him.

We saw him, my husband and I, at last; and we were together. I would have entered as a suppliant, but Hubert raised my hand to his lips and then placed it on his wrist, raising that high.

'I will escort you in like the royal princess you are,' he said. 'Between us we can overcome this matter.'

Henry was enthroned, wearing his crown; beneath it his golden hair had been curled and dressed becomingly. He had grown a beard, which increased the narrowness of his features. His lips smiled, but his eyes remained cold.

He mentioned Meggotta at once, saying he had made arrangements for a foreign bride for Richard. Foreign brides were much in his mind since the Poitevin alliances and his own betrothal, at last, to Eleanor of Provence, one of the three marriageable daughters of the prudent Count Raymond

Bérenger. None of them had any money, but one was already queen of France and much under the rule of her mother-in-law Blanche. I remembered all this while I listened to the king. Then I spoke out, as the Scots are inclined to do; we have never been a subtle race or apt at perfidy.

'Sire, it is too late, for my daughter and the earl of Gloucester are married,' I said. 'Do not blame my husband here, for he knew nothing of it, being in prison. It was I who made the marriage between them, as they had an affection for one another besides much shared land.' I thought it as well to say everything.

Henry smiled on. 'The pair are young enough for such a union to be set aside,' he said. 'It is not my will that the marriage should be made fact.'

'Sire, it is done.'

'You mean they have lain together?' Hubert had asked the same question, but differently. I could see his glance slide round, suddenly a man in fear. I do not know why this was so; perhaps armed men waited behind the curtain. The king was silent, which was worse than if he had broken out in one of his rages.

'I knew nothing of it,' I heard Hubert say.

The king rose in silence and withdrew, his robe trailing. I heard myself babbling like a guilty woman, saying what should not have been said aloud there.

'The king's father lay with his mother when she was eleven years old, and this Provençal bride of his is hardly older. Why should blame come to my pair, or scandal? My daughter is like to die of grief and shame if she cannot return to her husband.'

'Come away,' said Hubert in a tired voice, as though the whole matter concerned somebody else. It was as though by my very words I had become a stranger.

11

An oak withstands many blows until one reaches the heartwood, after which it no longer stands firm, and may soon fall. That blow had come to my husband when, seeing the king's reception of my news, he knew that whichever way the wheel of his own fortune might turn, Meggotta was ruined. He loved the little creature, had even disinherited his son for her sake; and now she was to be made a mockery by the world. He foresaw it all, that day. Thereafter he was courteous to me, and no doubt forgave me as far as it might be done; but matters between us were never again the same.

We spent the next two years, with our daughter, in a state of dread, never knowing when the blow would fall, except that it must. The king omitted no matters of vengeance, letting them ferment in his mind over a long time. He was so determined on his own will and sovereignty that even law and reason did not prevail. Despite what he knew about Meggotta's and Richard's marriage, he still tried to arrange a foreign one for the young earl with the queen's Provençal kin when she came; that plan however failed.

Gossip grew great about court, where we seldom now came. I suspect my stepson Bardolf, who had been much in Richard's company at Bury, for starting it. Another possibility was Richard's mother, whom he would certainly tell. She would in turn tell her husband the king's brother, and so it went on and round; though Richard of Cornwall was no enemy to Hubert, or a troublemaker.

Cognatus, of course, would go straight to the king on the matter, whether or not by way of Bardolf; since his mistaken support of Prince Louis in 1216 he had been zealous to prove his return to loyalty in all possible ways. However two things occurred about then to divert his full attention; one was the birth, at last, of an heir to him by the Marshaless. The other was her death soon after, and pompous funeral.

Cognatus named his heir John, the first de Warenne heir to be other than William since before the time of Hastings. No doubt he felt that having changed his own name back from Plantagenet, he had best atone.

These matters delayed the storm which burst again over my husband's head in 1236. Meantime, Meggotta was pining for hers. When they came together that time at Hertford, when she laid her soft young mouth against Richard's set one, she had been like a flower, perhaps the rose Hubert had described; now, she drooped, not even asking any more when she might see Richard again. I was troubled about her health; I tried as before to interest her in other matters to keep her spirits from flagging, as had succeeded at Bury in sanctuary. It was less easy now. A single night together was not enough to fix one girl's memory in the mind of the sought-after young courtier the earl of Gloucester had become. That Meggotta had that single night to remember might, for her, be all; but this I never breathed, only watching the sad time pass for her and, God knows, for myself.

It was in the autumn of that year that the barons indicted Hubert in the king's court. Henry himself was in the north, and sent for my husband to come to him at a place belonging to the Templars. It is called Eagle, and is in the flat Lincoln country. I can picture the narrow-faced king seated there, waiting for prey. On my husband's entry, Henry at once accused him of deceit over the marriage and of oath-breaking. He also stated that Hubert had forfeited the lands held under the agreement that the marriage should not take place. Hubert said again that he had sworn in good faith and that the lands should not be involved. He had a right to the constableship of Dover by charter, and as regarded the others he seemed able to satisfy Henry by the end, I did not ask in what manner. Certainly the three castles in Gwent were retained. We sometimes lived there.

A shameful agreement was reached after the king's marriage. Richard of Cornwall was party to it, and had given credence to de Lacy. The latter had gained the Lincoln title and now oftered his daughter to Richard de Clare as a bride. This was to be if failure of a more prestigious union to one of the daughters of Hugh de la Marche, by the dowager Queen Isabelle, came to nothing. The whole business was a market with souls for sale, and broken hearts. A date closing the bargain one way or the other was to be kept to by the following January.

Meggotta was dead by November, however. The king meantime pardoned de Lacy a debt of 2,000 marks.

I cannot bear to think of that slow dying, that awareness, of a young life that it could not longer be lived for any reason. I had of course fought the matter; how I fought it, and made my daughter fight also, at the queen's crowning! There were other scandals soon, other deaths; the papal legate was called in to settle the matter of Simon de Montfort and his forsworn anchoress and bride, the king's sister, Eleanor; even the emperor Otto, who rivalled Stupor Mundi except in marvels, was called in to arbitrate and to help. Help for us, for my husband and my daughter and myself, was not as readily forthcoming; except in one respect, and too late. The time came soon when I was no longer the next heir to the throne of Scotland, a fact which had made me dangerous, likewise my daughter, perhaps even Hubert still. My brother Alexander's barren English queen died in 1237. He was free to marry again and get himself a son.

To divert my mind I will describe the king of England's own nuptials, which had taken place two years before.

12

Henry III remained, as far as any of us knew, a virgin at the age of twenty-eight. Unlike his parents he was chaste as a part of his religion. However he had sought almost frantically for a wife after being denied my sister Marjory, and at the time of which I write had almost got himself two brides at once, being loath to part with one till he had secured the other.

The delay was the fault of Blanche of Castile, by now dowager and ruling power in France for her young son Louis IX. Louis's father, who had once invaded England, had only reigned three years. His widow was still the formidable early choice of Eleanor of Aquitaine, with an additional streak of Spanish cruelty disguised as religious probity. She was jealous of her rights to the extent of obliterating those of her son's young queen, Marguerite of Provence, who was only permitted her husband's company in bed to fashion heirs. The saintly Louis – he went to confession twice daily – had commenced his marriage by delaying consummation for three nights to mortify the flesh. All this was somewhat hard on the young bride, who by the end, after some years' delay, brought him eleven children. This brings me to King Henry's bride, for in the end he married Marguerite's sister.

Blanche of Castile had delayed a proposal of his to Brittany, as she decided, perhaps rightly, that that would give England a foothold again nearby the shores of France. The same thing happened in Ponthieu, where as I have said already the king of England had gone so far as to exchange informal vows with young Joanna. He had also sent to the pope for permission regarding consanguinity, which sooner or later can always be traced for the purposes either of marriage or divorce, everyone by now being related to everyone else in the same circle of high-ranking matrimonial exchange. Subsequently Henry changed his mind. This left Joanna of Ponthieu threatened personally by the French king's mother in a way that hardly bears out Blanche's vaunted piety. I do not share the general obsequious admiration of that woman; her character has been borne out by that of her youngest son, Charles of Anjou, whose cruelties are already notorious.

Blanche's unfortunate daughter-in-law Marguerite was the eldest of the three daughters of the penniless Count Raymond Bérenger of Provence, whose lands nevertheless gave access to the Midi and the Alpine passes through which merchandise might come, or armies defile into Italy. It is probable that Henry our king, who continued despite all lack of encouragement to hope to regain the Angevin empire of his grandfather, thought a Provençal marriage might give him access to the desirable lands once owned by Eleanor of Aquitaine, also to the heart of France itself. No doubt Queen Blanche would have made as good a soldier, had he essayed this, as she had in the days of her late husband's English venture. However when Henry made a proposal for the second sister Eleanor, perhaps finding her very name sympathetic, Blanche allowed matters to proceed; after all, she had firm control of Marguerite.

Henry had prudently had Eleanor surveyed and had been assured that she was beautiful. Beauty was necessary to him, in churches and in a wife.

The count sent hardly any money with his daughter, merely an abundance of needy relations. England became crowded with more Provençals than she ever had with Poitevins, who however remained and were hardly amenable to the newcomers. Feuds arose, but I anticipate. The queen's uncle, Peter of Savoy, was made guardian of Cognatus's young son, the seventh earl, Cognatus himself dying appropriately within five years. However before that there had been the royal wedding at Canterbury; and as countess of Kent I was bound to attend, with my daughter as countess of Gloucester.

It will be argued that this was cruel to Meggotta. No doubt that was so, and I suffered with her; but to fail to be present in her proper place would have been to give credence to the rumours that she was no more than Earl Richard's discarded child whore. The marriage had nevertheless been one in truth, and the world must know it. So I told her, and told Maud to set out our fine gear.

Meggotta had been quiet since Richard was taken away

into the king's wardship. I knew her sadness, but my, own spirit would have led me to fight; though doubtless by doing so I had already done only harm. As it was, I laid a gold-brocaded cloak on my daughter's thin shoulders, and bade her look at herself in the burnished mirror. I had combed out her hair.

'You are the countess of Gloucester, and I am the countess of Kent. We will don our coronets when the queen is crowned, and at the wedding we will be present with the rest of the nobility of England. Hold your head up; remember that your father also has had lies told about him, and has been mistreated. Your blood is royal, as good as the king's and better than the queen's.' So I talked to her; and she said neither yea nor nay, but presently asked if Richard would be there.

'I know not, and it does not matter. Behave with dignity, as befits your station, and nothing will go amiss.' I made ready fur linings for our cloaks, for it was just after Yule when Eleanor of Provence landed at Dover with a great company. The king rode to meet her there, but we did not; instead, we went straight to the church.

It blazed with candles and bright banners, in readiness for the marriage. I did not proceed to the tomb of St Thomas like most, as I have never forgotten how he caused the Lion's capture by raising a mist in Northumbria. I went instead, with Meggotta, to kneel at the tomb of St Alphège, the earlier archbishop who was done to death most horribly by the Danes. His body was revered for a long time in London before being stolen out of a window of St Paul's by King Cnut in person, and conveyed to Canterbury with great honour by water. I prayed to him that Meggotta's unhappiness might be ended, and that my husband might recover his health of mind. He had spent longer in gaol than the Saxon archbishop, whom they had held seven months in a longship before battering him with bones hurled from their feasting, when a convert gave him the *coup de grâce*.

The royal procession entered presently and we rose. From outside came the cheers of the people. The young queen – she was only twelve – was dwarfed by her tall husband, but her hair, like his, shone brightly in the light of the candles that day of January. As a grown woman Eleanor of Provence would be beautiful; even as a young girl her eyes were shrewd. She assessed us coolly as she passed by. Henry himself stared ahead.

In the procession walked Richard de Clare. He must have seen us standing by the shrine, Meggotta and myself; but gave no sign that he knew us.

I had grasped Meggotta's arm to support her; she was almost fainting. It was more than two years since she had set eyes on Richard. The longing in her face was piteous. 'It will soon be done,' I heard myself say.

The royal couple took the vows, exchanged their rings, and processed out after the nuptial mass. Several ladies of the court followed the procession. They did not address us, but I saw one nudge another, as much as to say 'There's de Burgh's daughter with her mother, the Scot. They say the young earl lay with the daughter, a feat at his age; he's older now, eh?'

They moved on, still talking and laughing. I squeezed Meggotta's hand to make no sign. She was as white as linen. 'He didn't see me,' I saw her lips move and say. If she thought that, poor child, it might aid her for the time.

We did not join the company after that, or see the king and queen bedded, but rode off with our own small following. The coronation at Westminster would be in six days, after much feasting. I determined, in spite of everything, that we would on no account be absent, and Meggotta should put on her coronet as I had vowed, when the queen was crowned.

13

As at the wedding, so at the coronation of the queen on 20th January. I was determined that the wife and daughter of Hubert de Burgh, himself again under restraint, should not be said to be ashamed to show themselves, should not submit to calumny.

The king had indulged, for the occasion, all his undoubted taste for splendour. The city was lit up against the early dark by a myriad candles and lamps. These were guarded and trimmed by servitors, some with staves. Hangings of coloured silk waved in the bitter wind, and banners with brave devices; the fesse checky of Warren and Surrey, which had lately superseded the old wyvern, stood out brashly in its azure and or. I had noted the Marshaless at the Canterbury wedding, and thought she looked ill; it was not long before we would hear of her death. The crowds pressed, kept in check by the constable of Chester, who had ridden south for the crowning.

It would, we already knew, be performed in the presence of

the king, wearing his regalia. I myself, as a princess of Scotland, wore my own light crown. My daughter, as countess, should put her coronet on her head immediately the queen was crowned. I already had a coronet of my own, set with pearls, which I carried ready for Meggotta. The king's almoner passed by, and the mounted citizens. They wore silk mantles worked with thread of gold, which shone in the lights, everything reflecting itself in the river, where lit barges swayed, making gleaming ripples. The king's trumpeters rode ahead of everyone, setting up a joyous blaring. The mounted citizens, I noted, carried each a gold cup, to present at the coronation feast. We would not attend it; but I remembered this privilege of the citizens of London from old days, and the king had with profit revived it.

A long blue cloth had been set at the Abbey door, and we walked up it to where two young men were arguing for precedence. One was Simon de Montfort, the other Bigod. Before them came three earls, and one was the earl of Gloucester. He still made pretence not to see us, but a muscle twitched at the corner of his mouth. I squeezed Meggotta's hand. 'He dare not look, sweetheart,' I murmured. Perhaps he had not perceived that she was beginning to grow little breasts, hardly yet noticeable beneath her gown. She stared with sad longing after him.

The treasurer followed, with the paten to be used at mass, bearing it carefully against his rich dalmatic. These had been introduced in the last century, by the last Queen Eleanor, who had been to Byzantium with her first husband Louis VII. Then came the chancellor with the king's chalice, a splendid thing of carved stone. Two knights carried sceptres for Henry and his queen, and then followed the king himself, his tall figure gleaming amid regalia, a purple silk canopy held above his head. It had silver bells and silver corner-lances, each held by barons of the Cinque Ports. I recalled the man who had saved Dover, whom the king had ordered to be confined in chains and in three rings of iron, instead.

Eleanor came then, walking gracefully beneath a second silk canopy, its silver bells tinkling like the last. She was escorted by two bishops. The Abbey was crowded to the doors; we ourselves, having arrived early, had a place near the front. There was much jostling to behold the new queen and to be noticed by her. She showed dignity and poise. It was evident that the king regarded her with affection and pride. I was glad for them despite everything.

The queen prostrated herself soon before the altar; there were prayers and singing, the blessing and unction of the coronation ring. *Christus vincit. Christus vincit, Christus imperat*, they sang. It had been the war-cry of the young Leper King outside Jerusalem, when he rode out alone to win the last Christian victory. There were lepers in the crowd beyond the doors now, threatened with burning if they caused harm.

The moment came when the crown was placed on the queen's head. I took the pearl circlet and set it firmly on my daughter's, I together with the other peeresses of England who raised their arms to do likewise. For moments Meggotta stood there among the rest, a countess for all to see. The young man who had denied her could not have failed to see her then also; I saw him flush where he stood nearby the king.

Perhaps he could not be blamed. Richard de Clare, like others, was in danger of losing all he possessed if he angered King Henry, even now. Maybe, I told myself in desperation, he was merely pretending to acquiesce; it could be that he would send word to us later. Nevertheless we did not follow the rest to the banquet. I would not touch a shred of Henry's venison, a crumb of his marriage-cakes, a drop of his wine.

When we regained my litter I saw Meggotta's face, and knew then that she would soon die, my daughter. Her eyes were closed as she lay back on the cushions, and the tears squeezed themselves from beneath her eyelids, rolling slowly down. She was silent; there was after all nothing to say. We made our way, without too much difficulty, back to our lodging; everyone was straining in the other direction towards the Abbey, waiting for the crowned pair to emerge.

I have never seen flesh fade from the bones in the way my child's did, in the months that followed. Within the year she was dead, at fifteen. I have somewhat more to say about her burial; but before she had been three months in her grave they married Richard de Clare to Maud de Lacy, the arrangements having been ready signed while Meggotta lay on her death-bed.

My husband's mind failed at Meggotta's death. After it he became a shell, as though his spirit had followed her wherever it had gone. I looked after him, by the end, and on his release, as though he were a child. He did not die till 1243, but in the last years there was nothing left between us except compassion and acceptance.

If therefore I speak of other matters at random, it is not that I forget. I have had to fill my own mind, my own life, with these, as dwelling on grief and nothing else drives one beyond sanity.

Matters with Scotland were unfriendly again by 1237, the year my daughter died. I had nevertheless determined to have her buried in the north, not in an England which had cast her out. Hubert at that time was still in prison, as I may not have made fully clear. His body's death came six years after.

I had arranged for Meggotta's bier to rest overnight at St Albans on our way north. Afterwards I gave the abbey a silk hanging in Hubert's name, in her memory. Few were present at the vigil mass except my sisters and old Maud, who wept uncomforted.

The candles flickered in the November wind, and I knelt close by the tomb of the protomartyr and thought how, like myself, he had almost certainly been a Scot. Alban is the old name for Scotia, long ago. King Malcolm Ceann Mór, my great-great-grandfather, was described in an ancient poem as the best king who ever ruled Alban. *He was a king of kings fortunate; he was the vigilant crusher of enemies.* Long before that, in the days of certain enlightened emperors of Rome, the Flavians, families living in the garrisons on the two great cross-country walls – the Romans never penetrated far into

Scotland – were allowed to worship as they pleased, Mithras or Christ. A son of such a family, gathered from either side of the wall, would be sent south in due course for military promotion; a soldier's occupation was then the only way for a young man of no particular birth or means to obtain any. Albanus, they would call him the southern garrison; no doubt he spoke with an uncouth accent and perhaps saw the ancient red carved stone portraying a Roman centurion spearing a crouching Briton, a design which has been adopted widely in England since to depict the legend of St George. Perhaps he saw it, perhaps not; but in either case he brought with him the knowledge of Christianity, and we do not know how that had arrived in Britain, and never will.

Alban was put to death under the son of Severus for protecting the Host. I have often enough ridden out to the place where he was taken, among trees near a stream. There is a stone altar there, and the legend is that Alban was executed for sheltering his friend Amphibilus. The word is said to mean a cloak, but to my mind means the great central enigma, the Body of Christ itself. I say little of such things, but they occupy my thoughts now till it is time to die. Then, at St Albans, I prayed for the soul of my daughter and that the young saint would lead her by the hand to God. Her time on earth had been short and her suffering great; perhaps she would be spared a part of purgatory.

The monks sang their dirges. I left them silver, and bade especial farewell to Father Lawrence, who had said the mass. I left with the light coffin carried along beside me and Maud in my litter; each time the road jolted I could hear the dead girl's head knock against the side. Father Lawrence had asked if I could not have her buried in St Albans, where I could visit her.

'No,' I said. I knew where I would take my daughter.

It was a long journey, and a cold one in the bitter wind and rain. I felt nothing of that, having long become a stone. I thought of death, but without desiring it for myself; till Hubert's release I must support him by my prayers, and later by such comfort as I could give. It was not yet, therefore, time for me to die.

At the border my brother the king's men waited, for I had sent word ahead. He himself was unable to come, being engaged in suppressing, in Galloway, a rebel named Gilrodh, one of the constantly recurring pretenders from the old Celtic line before Ceann Mór's Saxon second marriage. Alexander sent a message to say that he hoped I would join him for Yule, when the trouble should be over. He added that he would pray for my dead child's soul.

The men he had sent guided us east to Kelso, through the ancient forests where hidden Culdee monks still lingered despite Margaret Atheling's long-ago Roman reforms. We came to Kelso, where her son King David had intended one of his nine new abbeys to become the resting-place of Scottish monarchs. There I had Meggotta laid to rest, among those whose blood was royal, like her own.

Long ago, almost a century since, mourning crowds who had followed the bier of Earl Henry, David's son, the heir to

Scotland, across the land, had come here to see him entombed. His body lay nearby. I knelt for a long time in prayer for Meggotta, and asked my dead grandfather the earl, as I had asked St Alban, to guide her to God. Then I rose and left them and went north-east to await my brother's return, seeing the places I remembered from my childhood before visiting, as I intended, my parents' separate tombs at Balmerino and Arbroath, at latest by the spring.

Alexander had aged, and there was grey in his hair. He had dealt with the rebel Gilrodh and had time to spare for me. Joan was away, as often happened, in the south. We had not encountered one another on the way, as hers lay to the south-west, to some shrine or other at Keynstan Tarrant in Dorset. I regretted that Alexander had not found more comfort in his marriage. He was not of the kind who would have made an unfaithful husband in the ordinary way, but to prove to himself that he was not the barren partner in the union, had fathered a little bastard daughter he had called after Marjory. She ran about his court freely, and he was fond of her.

Something was however troubling my brother the king apart from the disappointment of his marriage, the recurrent turbulence in Galloway and Moray, and the late attempts of the king of Norway to take over the long arm of Kintyre. I knew that Alexander had remitted some matter to his confessor, but after that, as if he could no longer endure it, he brought it to me.

'I had to kill a little child,' he said. 'She was younger than Marjory. Had I not had her killed, had I even brought her here as hostage rather than prisoner, there would have been war in the end, for her cause; she was the last of the line of the second Duncan, who was murdered long before our time; but Gaels have long memories, and they would have married this girl to some man, even some king abroad, who would in the end have made war on her behalf; and I have had war enough.' He turned aside, so that I could only see his sturdy upright form and the back of his greying red head. 'I will never forget the sight of her blood on the ground,' he said. 'It was like the Holy Innocents, and I am Herod. God will curse me for it; had I a son he would be accursed also.'

'You had to do it for the sake of peace in your kingdom,' I said, knowing he always thought first of the welfare of his subjects; on the whole his land was peaceful and prosperous, corn growing to ripeness unburnt in the fields, even the matter of Northumbria agreed on with Henry III at last for the annual rent of a soar hawk, which let the Scots use Berwick. Henry, in fact, owed my brother money, which Alexander knew well enough he would never see. The extravagance of Queen Eleanor's kin spent it fast, in London. I comforted my brother as well as I could for the death of the child, but knew he would never forget.

Within a few weeks I left the court at Edinburgh and journeyed north to visit the Lion's grave. This was in his own foundation of Arbroath, the abbey which he had, curiously, dedicated to St Thomas Becket. The sea howled with spring gales, and the bulk of the great new abbey rose against its grey heaving and the sight, beyond, of the De'ils Heid. The abbot had had word of my coming and was waiting to greet me, but after a few words with him I said I wanted to go in by myself.

The tomb stood before the high altar. The Lion rested in peace, wrapped, they said, in the mantle of the religious order which caused him to be remembered abroad as William the Holy. He would have smiled grimly again had he still known. I knelt for some time by the tomb. Had St Thomas restored Scotland's freedom at Canterbury, in the time of Coeur de Lion, as a token of gratitude for this great abbey erected in his name? Was that why the Lion had founded it? No answer would be given me in this life, but I recalled that my unregenerate sire had mended his ways in the end and had even received the pope's Golden Rose, gleaming with sapphires, a high honour and sign of approval, seen already by me long ago.

Above the tomb hung a relic more holy than any; the Brecbennoch, the royal banner of Columba himself. It was very old now and threadbare, its colours long faded; but was to be revered as having been carried before the great saint when he journeyed to visit St Kentigern in the latter's green valley by the Molendinar, or else travelled among the heathen Picts, converting them. They say that when he was dying at last on Iona, a very old man, he ran like a little child to the altar to give up his life there, and a great light filled the church. He was kind to animals, and for this alone I have always loved him.

Now, I asked him to free my husband. I was aware, at the Lion's very tomb, that I was heard, that a voice already spoke to me; it did not mention Hubert, but a strangeness overcame me, and it was as if I heard the words *Something brave and noble will happen in this place.* It was in some way expressed in the inheritance of the Lion, in the standard, the great device itself. That hung above my father's tomb, alongside the Brecbennoch.

I left and rode south again to Balmerino, to visit my mother's tomb also. She had loved that place, as it was within the sound of the running Tay, and mother was a true Norman in that she liked the nearness of water. We had all come, in the first place, as pirates from the sea.

I lit a candle for her among the many that burned, and was pleased to find that chantreys for her soul's weal had been made by several knights who had known her in life. The quiet Queen Ermengarde had been quietly loved, even by my father in the end. She had borne her son late; I myself, even now, would never bear one; and I was still the heir to Scotland.

I crossed the Forth again then, feeling the sharp spring winds grow cold, reviving me. They blew nevertheless from the south; and on them I heard the sound of a passing-bell.

I heard the news soon. Joan of England was dead. My brother Alexander could marry again. I thought of his face, lined by now between nose and mouth, and the grey in his red hair; but he could still father a son. I fear I thanked God for poor Joan's death, and rode the faster once I knew for certain why the bell had been tolled.

*

I said nothing of that to Alexander, who mourned his sullen queen with propriety. Nevertheless freedom of my own from possible queenship, and my husband from the taint of false ambition, heartened me. I knew King Henry would have heard the news first, for his sister had died in Dorset, I do not know of what cause: and was buried there.

All of the king's half-brothers and sisters, and their husbands, who could contrive it came to the requiem. Among them was a mature man with grey hair and the unforgotten long limbs of the Lion. He exclaimed at the presence of Maud, who had come in behind me; and in the porch itself embraced her.

'Mother! My mother! I had not thought we would meet again in life.'

It was Robert of London, father's son, known for his benefactions to churches. Maud was trembling, and the tears coursed down her wrinkled cheeks.

'My boy Robert, my own boy. I had not thought we would meet more. You are grown a fine man since your father took you away on his saddle-bow, long since, long since.'

In the end it was arranged that she should stay with him, cold as Scotland was. At her great age journeying was in any case too much for her, though she had supported me valiantly. I would miss her, and gave her silver and thanks before I left. One more old friend had gone.

*

Lacking Maud, I made haste back to England after the requiem, at which I had knelt beside my brother. On the way home I paused for a night at what had been my uncle David of Huntingdon's palace. It was far changed, its master John le Scot being shabby by nature. His wife loathed him. They also were childless. I was glad to be back at last at Westminster and Woodstock, awaiting news of my own dear lord; but still there was no word, nor was he allowed speech with anyone.

I saw the queen, who had great influence with her husband although she was not yet pregnant, being still young. She received me alone in her newly painted room, and was a brilliant sight, in a jewelled coronal, a round shape Eleanor had lately made fashionable. She listened to me, and I saw that her eyelids were swollen by nature, giving a wise look older than her years. She promised to do what she could, but no doubt knew well enough with what manner of husband she dealt. A little later an assassin came into the palace, trying to kill the king; he was in some way connected with the Mariscos and the Marshal murder. Henry, who had heard him raving earlier in the day and had pardoned him, was sleeping with young Eleanor and not in his own bed, which saved his life. Had it not been for that, Richard of Cornwall would have become king of England, and would have shown mercy to my husband. As it was, Hubert's trial was not to be reopened for two further years. I forget how I spent them.

14

The fortunes of Cognatus, sixth earl of Warren and Surrey, had earlier neither waxed nor waned; he kept steadily in the king's favour, and though he had his heir he lost his wife. I did not attend the Marshaless's pompous funeral at Tintern, in which her four sons by two marriages bore the dead woman's bier with full panoply. The youngest, John de Warenne, soon now to become seventh earl, was carried in his nurse's arms while he grasped the fourth corner of the richly covered catafalque. He was able to stagger on his own feet by the time of the heart-burial at Lewes, which I attended by invitation.

I looked at him with interest, envying Cognatus his son; a fine fierce child, with the blood in him of Marshal, de Warenne and Plantagenet. Whatever the future might hold, John Warren would wield a sword in it.

Cognatus of course was draped in mourning, but the fesse checky blazed still. It diverted me, even in my sad state about Hubert, that so conventional a personage as the sixth earl should stress this, as it was a reminder of one of the scandals of last century, when the second earl had eloped with the wife of the not yet quite dead Beaumont earl of Leicester. She had been Isabel de Vermandois, already mother of five and the cousin of the king of France. It was she who had brought the fesse checky into the de Warenne family, and personally I would have kept it to one small quartering and the less said the better. However Cognatus knew how to make the most of his high descent, and by now few asked questions.

We passed, within the priory church of Lewes, the recumbent effigy of Cognatus' mother, pretty Countess Isabel, who had rebuilt the famous Cluniac foundation laid down soon after Hastings. I stared across at her quiet face carved in marble, and wondered how she liked being entombed forever close by her second husband, whom she had been forced to marry, in order to keep her vast estates in Normandy and England under the crown. The husband had been Hameline Plantagenet, a bastard brother of Henry II, and he was said to have become, in old age, a benefactor to many churches, no doubt being anxious for the welfare of his soul. His son, as I said, had disowned his surname, rightly considering his mother's the older.

We processed to the high altar, before which the heart of the late Marshaless was duly laid in its ornate casket. Other de Warenne hearts had been thus bestowed; one was of the third earl, Countess Isabel's father killed long ago in the Holy Land; but his quarrelsome wife was interred elsewhere, I think in Normandy; she had had de Bellëme blood and had fallen out with the prior and most others.

The carved capitals were very beautiful, portraying the miracles of Christ. There was an infirmary attached to the church which was famous for its healing. I went out into the sunlight at last with the company, and up the hill to the castle. On the way I wondered if Cognatus would marry yet again, and if so to whom; but in fact as I have said he died shortly, leaving young John as earl in the charge of Peter of Savoy, the queen's uncle, in Peter's new palace built by the Thames.

As I have also said before, the court itself by now was full of feuds between Provençals and Poitevins, but the king and queen seemed given to domesticity, and it was said soon after that that the queen was pregnant. Also, Henry planned to rebuild the Confessor's abbey of Westminster, and there was no doubt he would make a fine thing of it. Perhaps, amid so much, he would have the mercy to set Hubert free.

15

My brother the king of Scots mourned his dead wife duly for one year, then looked about for another who would give him an heir. He married, in mid-May 1239, an elegant French lady, daughter of a most powerful noble, Count Enguerrand III de Couci. Maric de Couci's father maintained a court more cultured than that of the king of France himself. The new queen of Scots brought with her poets, troubadours and sculptors and painters, also a knowledge of fine clothes and how to wear them. The Scottish court took on a new aspect. The fashion was for broad hats with flowing veils, which greatly became my brother's wife. She and he dealt well enough together, although their wills clashed on one occasion; but she made him an intelligent and lively companion, and, better still, in September of 1241, there was the birth of a splendid heir. He was christened Alexander.

Perhaps for that reason Hubert my husband, by then, had been freed and allowed to retire to his Essex manor, there to gaze into nothingness. First, however, there had been the reopening of his trial.

*

I am unable to this day fully to understand the mind of Henry III. Our castles in Gwent had been restored for three years before he changed his mind again, and for the third time brought my husband to be tried. Henry should have been secure by then: his young queen was with child, he had enough money and was his own master. What he feared from a broken old man I know not. He was rid of Peter des Roches and could afford to be generous, but by nature he was mean. He revived the supposed breaking of my husband's oath at Gloucester regarding the marriage of Meggotta, despite the fact that Richard de Clare was married again according to the king's will, and Meggotta herself two years dead.

My husband was brought in slowly on the arm of Father Lawrence of St Albans, who was his advocate. The sight of Hubert moved me more than I can say. Not only was his hair white and his gait shaky; his very gaze wandered vaguely, and at sight of me did not seem to know at whom he looked. I withheld my tears; they were of no value to anyone.

The charge was repeated, and the old trial of 1236 resumed where it had been left off. The charges of 1232 were also reopened, judgment never having been pronounced as there had been no plea. At that time certain of the earls had intervened on Hubert's behalf. Now, it was not politic for anyone to do so. Father Lawrence started the speech for the defence, when my husband suddenly rose from the chair where they had placed him, strength having been sent by God. As he had done long ago with Peter des Roches, he pointed a finger at the king.

'I have never been a traitor to you nor to your father, as is clear by God's grace in you.'

It might have been a man made young again. His voice was clear. Henry, taken aback, replied by a flood of coarse insults. The July sun flooded in. As is inevitable, in the end the king's side won.

However my lord's calmness and patience in the face of much abuse, and the fact that he was old, grief-stricken and ill, no doubt stood in his favour. He was allowed at last to keep certain castles, in other words enough room in which to die. The king graciously pardoned him for the regrettable first marriage of Richard de Clare.

As for the succession of what remained to us both, it is an irony that it was granted in the first place to our common heirs. Such is the law of England. Failing those – God knows, one had already failed – the lands were to go to Hubert's son John by his Bardolf marriage. The title of earl of Kent was to end with my husband's life; but we were permitted to retain the services of five knights, in the king's army, in Wales.

I looked at my reflection in my burnished mirror about then, and saw an old woman with grey hair. Meggotta should have inherited the Marcher lands, those of Essex and Peverel, Montgomery and Cardigan, Carmarthen and Gwent. She would have brought her young husband a further earldom and, at that time, the possibility of the kingdom of Scotland for their issue through myself. Now, all was ashes, except that our two lives, Hubert's and mine, remained.

III

1

King Henry's young queen did her duty and in the fourth year of their marriage, gave birth to a fine prince. I was permitted to visit the Lord Edward in his cradle, and as at Arbroath, at my father's tomb, a strange feeling overcame me.

Outside bonfires blazed, bells rang in every English town, and everyone rejoiced, although at the expensive christening it had been said sourly 'God gave us the child, but the lord king sells him.'

For me, it was different. I beheld a plump-faced, healthy baby, with fair hair and round eyes, whose left lid drooped like his father's. There was nothing as yet amiss; and yet a voice said to me *Smother this child in his cradle.*

Why had I heard so monstrous a thing in my mind? Was it a kind of vengeance on Henry III for what he bad done to my husband and daughter? It was more, I knew; and less as concerned the present than the future, like the bravery foretold in time to come at Arbroath. I did not obey the message;

I turned away. What would have become of me had I killed the prince did not matter; by then, my husband no longer recognized my face.

Those last years of Hubert's life were nothing, a void. Adversity had broken him, and though I always gathered news and related it to him as if he understood, he gave no sign. At news of the prince's birth he however turned his head aside, as if it no longer concerned him. As time went on he had to be fed like a child, with a spoon and cup.

Part of my news was of interest, nevertheless. In the next year the king's brother Richard of Cornwall, whose wife Richard de Clare's mother had died of childbed jaundice, made haste to marry Sanchia, the remaining sister of Queen Eleanor. That made a wily settlement by Count Raymond Bérenger for all his daughters; two were queens and Sanchia soon might be even more, as there were feelers from Germany and much strife among her rulers.

One cause of this was Stupor Mundi, the emperor Frederic II, and his quarrel with the pope. As usual the weapon of excommunication was used against him, and most harshly in his instance as he had newly taken Jerusalem, his cherished dream. This strange and gifted man had many dreams, and some had become reality; a university in Naples, reform of law, discoveries in science in which our Scottish wizard, Michael Scott, look part as Frederic's astrologer. All this gave an unforeseen wedding night to Henry III's sister Isabella, who had ridden to her marriage with cooking-pots of silver and much fine gear. On the night of the ceremony, the emperor, having earlier professed himself delighted with her witty conversation, came in briefly, performed the marital act once, then rose and told his bride she would bear a son in nine months precisely, as it had been already calculated. He then returned to his favourite mistress Bianca. Like my father he had a family of bastards, and like the kings of England a passion for hawking, on which he wrote a book. As for Isabella, she disappeared into his harem and did bear a son on the predicted date, who will not however inherit if indeed he still lives. At the time of which I am speaking the emperor was greatly troubled by the papal confederacy with Italian and German allies, as he had wanted to reduce the papacy to a mere archbishopric and assert his own authority over half Europe. In the midst of all these plans Isabella died, and another son roused German rivals including, I believe, the opposing emperor Otto, who had lately taken the part of Princess Eleanor, Marshal's widow, and Simon de Montfort following their scandal, which ended after all in happy marriage.

A lesser death than poor Isabella's occurred in that year, 1241; that of another Eleanor, the unknown Pearl of Brittany, true heir to the English throne. I did not tell Hubert Arthur's sister was dead; he was by then nearer Arthur in spirit than myself. This second Eleanor had had no freedom since the death, long ago, of old Eleanor of Aquitaine, her grandmother, who had at least taken her about after she was brought to England, having been reft from her mother, my niece Constance. The girl rode about then, had a saddle bought for her, and even once again crossed the Channel, much guarded. However after the old lady's death she was immured either in Gloucester castle or Amesbury convent, and seen by few; a plan to marry her into Austria came to nothing because of the Angevin ambition to suppress all dangers to the crown, One person who did see her, after her silver-gilt hair had long turned white, was the young waiting-woman, who had saved King Henry's life the night the assassin came, by screaming that he was in the palace with a knife. Her name was Margaret Bisset. She told me the Pearl of Brittany must once have been very beautiful. Now she was dead. I often wonder how she passed her days, except in waiting to die.

It seemed that my own life had also been lived in vain, except that I had known great love from my husband and for my daughter. Now I never ceased to pray constantly that one day, in some manner, Hubert would again know who sat by him, told him such news as came, tended him and helped to feed him, holding the cup to his lips, guiding each ready spoonful. It troubled me particularly that I was then still heir to Scotland, Alexander's queen not having yet conceived. As before, if anything befell amiss I must go, and take Hubert with me, no longer a wise aid and counsellor but an old man past knowing either peace or war. I would not leave him to the wolves; where I went he should come also; but my grandmother Ada the Countess had governed Scotland wisely as a free widow, not with an invalid to tend who took much tending. Certainly, my brother had laid down a strong clear pattern of rule and all I need do, if let, was to follow it. However even he had had to contend with rebels, and so had Ada de Warenne. The future held a certain hope: but it had been thus in the days of the old Tanist inheritance, no doubt for the reason that with constant wars between clans, only women were left to bear.

All this fear of the future was in any case rendered pointless. That Yule, after the queen of England had borne a daughter they named Margaret, not for myself but for her sister the queen of France, Queen Marie of Scots conceived. My brother's splendid son Alexander was born in early autumn. I was told he had red-gold hair.

I longed to ride north and behold my nephew for myself, but Hubert still lived on. It was not for two more years that I was freed by his death; how little I would have expected to use such a word formerly!

He died at his manor of Banstead in 1243. I was with him, and he did not know me till the last, when every sense but hearing had gone. He could no longer mumble a confession to the priest, who gave him conditional absolution; and after that, though no one is supposed to approach the dying absolved lest they sin again, I came and knelt by Hubert and took his hand. He still lived, but he was ebbing fast. I said close against his ear 'My husband, if you have forgiven me and know I love you, press my hand.'

His eyes turned slowly, almost with suspicion, to me; I

knew he had heard but could not speak. His hand then pressed mine, and within moments he had gone from me. I looked down on his dead face and watched the lines fade till it was smooth and clear again, the face God would see, and God knows all. Then I turned away and let them do those things which must be done to the dead, before burial.

After my husband's body had been entombed among his Dominicans, the Black Friars, in London, I rode north to see my royal nephew Alexander, and to embrace his father once again.

2

It might have been said that I had no reason ever to return to England. My brother would have welcomed me in Edinburgh for as long as I cared to stay; the little curly-haired prince was a delight, already cutting his teeth and showing charm and intelligence beyond any child I have known. His father doted on him, and the pleasure of watching the king's face lighten, as Hubert's had used to do with Meggotta, out of loving care, his son on his knee, talking of the pony young Alexander should soon learn to ride, showing him with pride to the folk of the town from his crupper when we rode among them, almost made me forget what I had left; empty manors, tenantless castles inhabited only by guards, with garde-robes and the chests wherein lay Hubert's clothes, unworn for years except for the night-gear of an invalid; his shirts and tunics and hose, the great cloak he had worn as Justiciar of England: memories of Meggotta. All these I had left behind, and nobody else cared for them; John, who had his full prospects of inheritance now except for the title, was heedless, never having forgiven his earlier displacing by my daughter.

I could have stayed, therefore, in Scotland; except for the queen.

Like most Frenchwomen Marie was shrewd, and did not altogether relish the prospect of my presence for longer than the time of an ordinary visit should take. She was always courteous to me, but the knowledge was there between us, unspoken of: nor, like most women, did she require her husband the king's attention to go to any other for long, even his sister. It was not that she loved my brother Alexander as I had loved Hubert de Burgh: in France a marriage is a contract between persons suited to one another, made after reflection and consultation, usually between parents. In England things are less considerate. Marie had carried out her duty as Alexander's wife and queen; she and he respected one another; and he was of course grateful for the magnificent son. I felt that I must leave them to their predicted and civilized happiness in the marriage and their child; so I came quietly home. Poor Marjory in any case, by then, was still mourning her earl, killed in the Hertford tournament in the year young Alexander had been born.

So I returned to England, remembering the king my brother's close embrace, and his warm invitation to ride north again whenever I chose. It was almost as though he had known he would never see me more. He had only six years left to live.

He died unexpectedly, in the summer of 1249, during a voyage to the Western Isles. He had been carried, in great pain, off the ship which had taken him to visit, and dine with, the Lord of the Isles to try to reach some agreement, and to obtain the control of the seas surrounding those coasts. There was possible treachery with Norway, and the island lords regarded themselves in any case as petty monarchs, as good as the king. Alexander had recently quelled Galloway by campaigns, and hoped to do the same in the Isles by a personal meeting instead. After it he was seized with pain and fever, and died soon on Kerrera, which is nearer the mainland he was never again to see.

I am aware that the sudden deaths of high personages is often blamed on poison, but I cannot help wondering if the king of Scots' fever was convenient to some, leaving a child to wear the crown; granted Alexander III had good advisers left by his father, but Scotland had lost a wise king.

I could only pray that Alexander III would have a long and peaceful reign, with none of the troubles with the English rulers his father, and my own father, had had; and besides ruling strongly for himself would have many sons from his marriage, whoever should be his bride. He would be taught courtly manners by his French mother. I knew Marie, a young woman, would no doubt marry again, and this has happened, but her second husband, Jean d'Acre, is a good stepfather to the boy. Also my half-sister Isabel's husband de Ros was one of the young king's guardians, and would see to it that his rights were not encroached upon. It is, at least a different situation from that in England, where the king is no longer beloved and his queen hated for her greedy relatives.

*

I was to see the young king of Scots, Alexander III, again at his knighting and his marriage. He was ten years old when Henry III knighted him at York on Christmas Day of 1251, and was married the day after to the little princess Margaret, just a year older than he. In the unforgotten Minster, as the two children exchanged their vows, the strangeness came to me once again, and I heard a voice, this time a young man's, tired as though he was dying. It said *This day the sun of Scotland will set.* I do not know what will happen in this way, or when. Till now, Alexander III has had a fine reign, and there are prospects of an heir now, as young Margaret is pregnant. They have ridden down to Windsor for the birth, which was unwise; but King Alexander is not so as a rule, and when he took the oath of homage as a child being knighted, he told the king clearly that his homage was only for the lands he held of him in England. Henry was not pleased. However there have been visits since then between them.

I am not well these days, and the matter of the young king of Scots' marriage brought what will no doubt be my last encounter with Richard de Clare.

3

I am more than fifty years old now, and have not been in good health. On most days, in this house of Hubert's by the Thames at Westminster, I lie on my day-bed, looking out and watching the swans, especially when the cygnets come and are brown and hesitant at first, then turn snow-white and confident. It gives me pleasure to watch them swimming with their parents, graceful at last, long-necked and proud. The river has seen many things, including the white-and-gold rising of the king's new abbey itself.

Two days ago a visitor was announced and I was astonished to receive the earl of Gloucester, and did so coldly. He was no longer the young Paris by now, but Hector the seasoned warrior. His face was still sunburnt from the visit to Germany to crown Richard of Cornwall king of the Romans and future emperor. Yet he did not look well, and told me he and his brother William had lately been poisoned by their steward. Richard recovered, but William died. 'One can trust nobody,' the earl said, and stared down at where I lay. He spoke with difficulty then, in a low voice. 'No doubt, madam, you have found me as untrustworthy as any. I do not forget your kindness to me while I was a child in your care, or my little companion then. You know that I have called one of my daughters Margaret. It was in memory of her.'

I raised my eyes to him. 'She would have needed no memorial had she lived,' I said directly, for I do not flatter. 'She died of grief from your unkindness.'

'I dared not be kind. The king could be vindictive in those days, and remarked everything. Now, only last year, Henry was made, as you know, to sign the Provisions of Oxford, wherein he is compelled to hold less unchecked power than formerly. Simon de Montfort and I, and other lords, have been at some pains to ensure it, and if necessary will take matters further, as Magna Carta did not go far enough. Your husband's treatment would not be permitted Henry now.'

'It is too late to tell me that; the earl of Kent is dead. Why, have you come?' I did not offer him wine.

'To tell you that I have undertaken many pilgrimages to atone for my sin in betraying Meggotta; to Pontigny, to Compostela and to Rome. I heard that you were not well, and wanted to pay my duty to you. I will go, as you do not welcome me.'

'I am glad that you have come,' I said more graciously, and asked how his wife and children fared. A little daughter had died, he said, two years ago. Of his three sons, Benet might enter the Church.

'Sit down,' I said. 'I am not so lacking in sinfulness myself as to hold it against others. Tell me your news; I last heard of the splendour of a Christmas feast you held in Wales.'

'Wales I have been to, but the tale I wanted to tell comes from Scotland, where I have also been, though not of late. Word came from the little Queen Margaret there that they were keeping her from the company of her husband till he was sixteen. I remembered only too well what had happened in my own case, and together with another knight made pretence to be part of the force of one de Ros, who was guarding the king and queen separately in Edinburgh. We threatened him, rescued the young couple and brought them south on a visit. They are friends as well as husband and wife. I would have told you earlier, but have been much abroad, firstly refusing to aid the king and later aiding his brother; also, my brother William needed aid in France while he lived, and received it, though I was much assailed by Frenchmen.'

He smiled, and, as long ago, I was aware of his charm. I did not say de Ros was Isabel's husband.

The earl talked then of the marriage of the Lord Edward in Spain, which he had attended; and of John, seventh earl of Warren and Surrey, who is at present busied in acquiring even more lands in England than even he ought to possess.

'It is of no point to argue with him, and when Edward returns from abroad he may do so; the pair are friends. All Warren does is to grasp his sword and say he has won all he has by it. *Gladio vincit, gladio teneo, gladio tenebo,*' he roars, and has taken *Tenebo* for his motto. You, madam, have de Warenne blood; you merit the term yourself well enough.'

He left me, and I lay watching the water and the swans again, somewhat freed of bitterness. Perhaps the end of life is always this, learning to watch and listen, and to accept fairly. I wonder what will be achieved by Simon de Montfort, who also has persuasive charm? It may be that justice will prevail in the end, in England. What will become of Scotland I do not know.

I am tired, and will sleep.